THE DEATH OF UNCERTAINTY

THE DEATH OF UNCERTAINTY

A STORY OF AI AND FREE WILL

MICHAEL TAN

NEW DEGREE PRESS

THE DEATH OF UNCERTAINTY

A Story of AI and Free Will

ISBN   978-1-64137-402-6 *Paperback*

978-1-64137-403-3 *Kindle Ebook*

978-1-64137-404-0 *Digital Ebook*

CONTENTS

ACKNOWLEDGEMENTS

Thank you to all those who have guided and supported me in this endeavor. Writing and publishing this book has given me much to be grateful for.

Special thanks to Professor Eric Koester, the team at New Degree Press, and Brian Bies, without whom this would not be possible.

Thank you to my editors Cortni Merritt and Elina Oliferovskiy, who have provided invaluable and thoughtful guidance and have dedicated much time and energy toward this book.

To my friends, who have cheered me on and provided me with fellowship and camaraderie. I will treasure and cherish our relationships for years to come.

And last but not least, thank you to my family and my parents, who have supported me from day one. I owe everything to you.

As for my personal supporters of the book, I want to thank:

Man-Lin Hsiao	Erik Jia
Nitin Sampath	Harry Wang
Gouttham Chandrasekar	Eric J Little

Lawrence Chen
Alex Balfanz
Aman Sawhney
Will Robbins
Vamshi Eppanapally
Karina Chan
Jacob Young
Yixin Lin
Rohan Datar
Josh Farahzad
Manasi Maheshwari
Joshua Jen
Dilan Trivedi
Shamikh Hossain
Felicia Lin
Aditi Gopalan
Jeffrey Li
Beini Yin
Aaron Kuo
Kevin Huang
Melissa Cai
Itamar Barak
Chiwan Kim
Rohith Kuditipudi
Gonzalo Pernas
Bolun Li
Qusai Hussain
Jade Davis
William Reynolds
Adit Madhavan

Ian Buchanan
Luke Qin
Edward Chen
Cipriano Echavarria
Shawn Luo
Thomas Williford
Michelle Yin
Jason Zhang
Kushal Kadakia
Hal Lin
Ritik Goyal
Colin Parsons
Ogni Goswami
Aneesh Deshpande
Victor Kao
Tony Wang
Patrick Lee
Arup Banerjee
Sophia Beyda
Han Zhang
William Min
Eric Dang
Eric Gan
Aamir Azhar
Lavanya Vijayan
Arsh Vishen
Benjamin Chen
Rishabh Swarnkar
Kaixi Yang
David Kobrosky

and many more for your direct support throughout much of the journey.

NOTES
FROM THE AUTHOR

———

As we prepare to enter the third decade of the twenty-first century, we're entering into a brave new world flush with unparalleled amounts of and access to data. I see many striking implications coming from this. On the less severe side, companies have been able to determine that a teenager was pregnant before her father could by mining shopping data. Darker applications include the use of data by companies like Palantir to profile individuals based on their predicted probability to commit crimes (just as in the movie *Minority Report*), or by governments such as China to enforce a social credit system that extrapolates from one's daily actions to evaluate and predict how "good" of a citizen one is. Indeed, these applications can have both benefits and disadvantages. For example, if data indicates that one has a high probability of committing a crime in the near future or that one is a bad citizen (by some government-determined metric), then institutions may proceed to act on the suggestions of the data by limiting the freedoms of the individual in question. This may lead to a safer, more productive society—yet, at the same time, this approach can lead to a slippery slope where data is used as a justification for the curtailing of individual liberties. This is the world we're entering. This is our future. Tomorrow's generations, from the Millennials onward, will live in this world. It can be dystopian—the stuff of science fiction stories—and the fear of a data-driven future has only been stoked by the channels of modern mass media.

But a data-driven society can also be seen as the pinnacle of a search for knowledge and truth that has lasted from the very beginnings of human society. Much of human history is the story of people trying to create ways to reduce uncertainty and make better decisions—in essence, to find truth. The pursuit of knowledge has benefited our human race greatly—no longer do we sit by cluelessly as a Black Plague kills a third of a continent as our medieval ancestors did, and no longer do we perish as a result of eating the wrong berry as our hunter-gatherer forebears did.

Yet, we still have much room for improvement. Decision making is still imperfect. But it doesn't have to be. In theory, in every set of decisions exists an optimal choice. With big data, it isn't so farfetched to imagine a world where the optimal decision can always be determined. For the first time, with our new access to hordes of data, the ultimate truth can be pinpointed more precisely than ever. Truth can prevail and serve as the basis for all decision making, and we'll finally be able to make perfect decisions.

With the advent of big data and machine learning, the probability that an outcome will happen, whether that be if a woman becomes pregnant or if a person will commit a crime, can feasibly be predicted with high accuracy in the near future. And once we reach the end of that search for truth, then we'll be the most informed people to ever live. In every case, an optimal decision can be found—there will be no more uncertainty about whether or not a choice is the right one. Data can determine for certain what's best.

But if we envision a world where we can know for certain what's optimal, then, in such a world, our ability to make suboptimal decisions will be taken away. In other words, free will and autonomy will be taken away as we all follow the predetermined optimal decisions that have been laid out for us by the data.

If free will is simply a means to achieve the end of good outcomes for ourselves, then is there a need for the means of free will once we find foolproof and accurate ways to achieve the end of good outcomes? Certainty relieves us of our free will, which, by its nature, relies on chance to present us with the illusion of choice. When we're uncertain of the outcome of our will, the pressure overwhelms the illusion.

And without uncertainty and free will, adversity is impossible. If every decision can be made optimally without any mistakes, then it will be highly unlikely that adverse situations can arise. Data-driven optimality could completely relieve humans of stress, inconvenience, and missteps, replacing them instead with luxury and comfort.

Is there value in adversity? Does it enhance life in some way, perhaps by enriching experience or contributing to individual growth? Is it purely a negative aspect of life that we'd be better without? And if the answer is the former, then how would individuals in a society that lacks exposure to adversity behave? If there's value in adversity, then is there also value in making suboptimal decisions?

These questions are important to directionally guide the application of big data technologies. It determines what these applications should optimize for. If the goal is perfect information, ultimate efficiency, and optimality, then we may just as well end up in a world of luxury and comfort, and lacking in adversity. We could create a hedonistic utopia where pleasure is maximized and pain is minimized. In many ways, one can see the history of mankind up to today as a pursuit of that very goal—maximization of pleasure and minimization of pain. Would such a thing be desirable? At first glance, it seems like the answer is yes. More of a good thing (pleasure) and less of a bad thing (pain) must obviously be good on net. But the question is more complicated than that, and this work seeks to develop an adequately nuanced answer.

Some other questions to be explored are as follows.

What exactly is the nature of free will?

What's the use of free will?

What's the value in suboptimality and adversity, if there is any?

What does it mean to be human?

What should be the goal of society?

These questions have driven me to create this work. To better answer these questions, I've drawn upon my background in statistical science and spoken to many experts in the Artificial Intelligence and Machine Learning fields.

To explore them, I've created a world with a data-driven machine that can optimally decide the best decision for any and every fork in the road. One would never make a wrong move ever again; one would only make the moves that the machine tells them to make. What would it be like if such a machine existed?

In my view, free will is the child of uncertainty, and a world without uncertainty is a world without free will. But is that so bad? For a world without uncertainty also means a world without suboptimality.

This book is for those of us who are interested in the philosophical implications of data, who enjoy ruminating on the nature of free will, and who are on the precipice of this data-driven utopia/dystopia—all of us.

CHAPTER I

———

6:20:24 a.m. For Viktor, this was the precise time today to awaken from his slumber. There were no two ways around it. A second less or a second more and the REM cycle wouldn't be optimized given the temporal constraints of his schedule. His cortisol would be higher than it needed to be and his oxytocin too low. 6:20:24 a.m. Perfect. For HAPOC had told him so.

The High-Accuracy Probability and Outcome Computer, or HAPOC, was the breakthrough technology of the twenty-second century. It did exactly what its name suggested—it rapidly and efficiently calculated outcomes and probabilities with high accuracy. With the unparalleled troves of data and information that humanity was given access to with the Second Scientific Revolution, HAPOC became the unquestioned reference to direct all action—it could factor in any imaginable input and produce as outputs potential outcomes and probabilities corresponding to certain paths of action. From these outputs, people would be able to make decisions with absolute certainty—and HAPOC was almost certainly right. After it had spent forty-two hours training itself and getting to know the ins and outs of the world, from the global economy to regional weather patterns, to the psychological biases and instincts of each of the 12 billion people on the planet, HAPOC could predict accurately without fail. It could sift through whatever chaos there was and find reason, for all things have their causes, and with its almost unlimited processing power, HAPOC could factor in every possible cause and produce all possible outcomes. It gave the best ones as recommended paths of action to its users.

HAPOC had guided humanity through the existential Climate Crisis of the late twenty-first century—its contributions included finding the optimal allocation of wind farms and solar panels and discovering a foolproof way to safeguard humanity from the downsides of nuclear fission. It had also given policymakers recommendations that effectively wiped terrorism off the face of the earth. HAPOC and its recommendations, when implemented, had solved almost every human problem in sight. The machine was always right, and to defy HAPOC would amount to nothing less than self-destruction. This was true, for HAPOC had said so.

Today, Viktor, like all other citizens, had used HAPOC to determine the best time to sleep and the best time to wake up. After all, it was mandated by the law of the City. HAPOC had used Viktor's unique biological data, down to his very genome, to calculate a precise, objective answer that would optimize the performance of his cells during the day. HAPOC knew who Viktor was better than he did—all of Viktor's desires, aptitudes, and thoughts were all a function of the neurons and chemicals in his brain—and HAPOC, by virtue of having complete knowledge of Viktor's biological makeup, could predict what desires and thoughts Viktor's neural system would likely generate.

So, at 6:20:24 a.m., Viktor dutifully woke up, having gotten the best night's sleep possible. With HAPOC's help, no one would ever wake up "on the wrong side of the bed." Besides, on the off chance that HAPOC got it wrong (this rarely ever happened), Viktor always had the option of getting a shot of oxytocin into his system, or of whatever he needed. Everything could be fixed, and everything had a right answer.

As a result of this perfect calculation, Viktor had no need to rub his eyes or feel groggy. Instead, he leapt out of his bed, which was also made perfectly for his body shape and idiosyncratic sleep habits. He stretched his muscles and made his way down to the bathroom, his bare feet touching the marble tiling that was used in almost every residence and workspace in the City. The marble wasn't cold at all, being heated to the prime temperature for the morning, so Viktor did not feel the cold sting that often comes from tiled floors.

Once in the bathroom, Viktor hopped into the bathtub and took his perfect shower. It was set at just the right temperature for his body, and warm water gently flowed onto his bare torso, hitting his skin with just the right pressure. Viktor's body, like everyone's, was in good shape—it was hard not to be when every aspect of life was optimized according to each individual's biological genome. It was healthy but thin. Scrawny but in good shape. He had no need for extraordinary strength.

Viktor went downstairs in his pajamas to greet his parents, as he did every morning. His parents had valued family togetherness very highly, and HAPOC told them how to achieve just that. Since he was born, Viktor had received biweekly doses of 5COM21, a chemical that stimulated the region of Viktor's brain that activated strong senses of compassion, loyalty, and obedience. His mother and father took 5COM21 themselves as well—they found it the perfect antidote to any possible marital spat or discomfort. They had the perfect family—everyone felt cared for by each other very much.

"How'd you sleep, son?" Viktor's father asked as he saw Viktor coming down the stairs.

"Perfectly. Couldn't imagine anything better," Viktor responded. And that was an objective fact—no other sleep could have granted him such optimal levels of energy and rejuvenation—HAPOC saw to that.

"Good, dear. Let's finish the morning routine then. There's some good cereal in front of you. Updated to work optimally with your digestive system and genetic makeup, now that your body is changing," said his mother.

"Thank you, mother," replied Viktor. He glanced down at the bowl of cereal in front of him. Filled to the brim with milk and flakes synthesized to contain the perfect combination of nutrients to fit Viktor's bodily needs, the breakfast food, like all food, was optimized for each person. It was prepared by machine, and the final product was delivered to the consumer. No more time was wasted on indecision over what to eat, for there was always a right thing to eat.

Viktor scooped up the cereal and put it in his mouth. It tasted wonderful. His taste buds burst with delight, for the flakes had activated all the right areas on his tongue.

"Mmm," Viktor murmured as his lips curled up into a satisfied smile. The cereal had given his brain a small dose of dopamine, a mechanism that would make Viktor want to eat more and be motivated to gain all the nutrients he needed. Viktor, pleased, took the bowl in one hand, raised it up to his mouth, and began to slurp the cereal in.

"I knew you'd like it." Viktor's mother smiled.

"You mean HAPOC knew. HAPOC's the real genius here," chirped Viktor as he continued to chow down the cereal.

"Fair. Is that a sly compliment to yourself?" his mother replied.

Viktor chuckled. "I just help out with the algorithm. Though it's great to learn from the seasoned engineers, who really deserve the credit for all HAPOC has brought us."

Viktor said it with a glint in his eyes. It was the societally appropriate thing to do, though he knew that his contribution to the algorithm was integral. Even at his tender age, Viktor was one of the smartest engineers, a bright young star, whose light the City sought to harness. His intellectual vitality was two standard deviations above the mean—Viktor took much pride in this knowledge, and HAPOC would routinely remind him of the fact.

Viktor's father chimed in. "Anything fun in store for us from HAPOC soon?"

"You'll see when it's out. You know my work is confidential," replied Viktor with a bit of playfulness in his tone. It was a subtle brag, a snarky comment that revealed both pride and insecurity in being so young yet already so valued by society, so much so that he was working on projects that required the highest security clearances.

"Well you have a good day at work; your father and I do have to get going to our jobs," his mother said as both parents got up out of their seats.

Viktor abruptly got up as well, and the three embraced. Embracing was good for the mental and physical health of the family. It kept the oxytocin flowing and the cortisol levels down. Thus, logically, the government had mandated that embraces were to be shared before each departure between family members.

With that, the parents left the house, and Viktor finished his cereal. He put his bowl in the sink and turned on the faucet to rinse it. The water flowed out of the faucet until it filled the bowl to the brim, and then Viktor emptied it of its contents. Small cereal residue flowed down into the sink, carried by the water, spiraling from a disorderly and chaotic mess into a singular point of order from which it disappeared into the sink, leaving both sink and bowl clean. With that done, Viktor placed the bowl into the dishwasher, a machine that cleaned soiled dishes with the use of new technologies like sound vibration and ultraviolet light.

Viktor had a big day ahead of him, and he was excited by it. It was time for work, that daily regimen that gave him purpose.

CHAPTER II

———

Today, like all days, Viktor prepared for a morning jog. His route of choice was a couple thousand revolutions of the treadmill machine they had in an exercise room in the house. Jogging in the morning was prescribed by HAPOC, and it always led, without fail, to him feeling ready for the day ahead. After all, exercise in the morning was proven to boost his serotonin levels and lead to a clearer mind and more motivated spirit.

Viktor went back to his room, changing into a pair of shorts and T-shirt, both meant for his use in recreational activities. They were tailor-made, personalized to his body, and allowed for free, aerodynamic movement as he ran. They were white with no designs and made of special sweat-absorbing fibers. The shirt hugged Viktor's body tightly, caressing his chest and torso. Viktor liked the fit. He liked the color too—simplistic and clean, a blank slate.

He went into the bathroom, a room with four white walls. In it was a toilet, a shower, a sink, and a counter with drawers. The counter was made of cold white marble, and upon it sat a cup that served as a holder for a high-tech sonic toothbrush and a tube of toothpaste. Beside that sat a case of hair gel, a bottle of cologne, some lotion, and some face wash. Next to that was an assortment of pills, manufactured solutions for enhancing the health of the human body. Viktor flicked the switch, flooding the room with white light.

Viktor checked his reflection in the mirror. Smiling back at him was a tall, slender young man in his late teenage years. Subtle signs of pubescence still were visible on his face—a small zit on the cheek, some scruff growing on the chin—but his jawline had sharpened, losing its baby fat, morphing into the face of a man. Above a pair of pale brown eyes were two perfectly pruned eyebrows. A bed of unkempt bedhead sat atop the head. This was also the face that HAPOC saw from its mechanical, glass eyes that were built into the mirror.

Viktor hadn't always been happy with how he looked, but now with the results of his puberty-induced transformation, he was more than satisfied. HAPOC had guided him through the process with personal grooming and style recommendations. Viktor had in him the vanity of youth, and HAPOC had catered to that vanity by making Viktor look as polished as can be. Growing up, Viktor had been more gifted in mind than body, but now he was a standout in both aspects. His insecurities had stemmed from this imbalance, but HAPOC had helped Viktor gradually correct it.

Suddenly, the mirror spoke. "Brush your teeth please," said HAPOC gently, noticing the bacteria on Viktor's tongue, both by smell and sight.

Viktor picked up his toothbrush, applied toothpaste, and vigorously brushed. After a minute, Viktor began to slow down and picked up his cup to rinse his mouth.

At that moment, HAPOC reminded, "For two minutes."

Viktor, realizing that he had been caught, continued brushing for an extra minute. He finished and rinsed, letting the water fill his mouth and gather up all the residue from breakfast before he spit it out. As with the bowl at breakfast, a chaotic swirl of brown, gnashed-up, nasty-looking food bits spiraled into a singular point of order in the center of the sink before disappearing.

Viktor smiled at the mirror again, and HAPOC tacitly took a detailed look at him and his teeth. The mirror, satisfied with the cleaner mouth it had guided Viktor to create, voiced that satisfaction, "Great! Brushing for two full minutes is key to dental health."

HAPOC was now ready to release Viktor. "You are ready to go to the gym!" HAPOC exclaimed.

So, Viktor made his way down the stairs and into the exercise room where the treadmill waited. He slipped his feet into the shoes that sat next to the treadmill. The laces tightened themselves around his feet, applying just the right amount of pressure and tightness. They were white. Viktor stepped onto the treadmill, and the machine began to move.

HAPOC spoke, "Let's start at a leisurely pace and speed up from there."

Viktor began to walk. This warm-up period was essential for loosening his muscles before he really got into the run. A minute passed, and the treadmill sped up.

"Get ready for a light jog!" HAPOC said encouragingly.

The machine adjusted itself to Viktor's every step. It monitored Viktor's heart rate and breathing to move ever so slower or faster, pushing him to the optimal level of exertion. It was a controlled environment, optimized also for safety. It knew when to automatically slow down when Viktor was getting tired. This way, Viktor would never fall or feel too strained. The treadmill was a cradle, a place for Viktor to embrace motion and incubate before he went off on his days.

So, Viktor ran, with each step releasing ever-increasing amounts of serotonin in his brain. Each step felt therapeutic, and each step landed on a platform that was configured perfectly just for that step. The right speed, the right gradient, the right resistance—all of it helped to rock Viktor into a comforting yet productive cycle of movement. The machine adjusted itself to allow for Viktor's own movements to become rhythmic and machine-like—a self-perpetuating cycle, a cradle that rocked back and forth to output the endorphins needed to make Viktor optimal.

Viktor, smiling as he ran, relished the thought of getting closer to optimality with every step. He was a man driven by a desire to achieve. As a youth, he had always thought of himself as one of the most talented, an assumption that HAPOC had only served to confirm with quantitative metrics. And this gift of intelligence had given Viktor the sense that he was destined to do something great with his gift. With this also came a fear that he would somehow waste it all. It gave him an almost ruthless level of rationality as well as a powerful motive to persevere until he reached his goals. With these tools in hand, Viktor had secured a position as an engineer working on HAPOC's algorithm—he was, in fact, the youngest ever person to hold such a job. He was a perfectionist and was absolutely dedicated to constantly growing and getting better both personally and professionally. Viktor ran every day so that he was ready to perform and would live up to the expectations that he was so afraid to fall short of. He smiled because he knew the running made him a better, more optimal person.

Viktor jogged, transferring force from the back to the front of his feet as he made contact, arms swinging in concert.

He did this for half an hour, breaking a cool sweat and feeling refreshed and ready for the day.

HAPOC confirmed the feeling, "Great job, Viktor! You're ready for the day. Just take your shower and get dressed for work!"

Viktor obediently went back up the stairs to his bathroom, took his form-fitting but now sweat-filled clothes off, stepped into the shower, and turned on the water.

It was cold at first—meant to further wake him up and make him more alert. Then it turned warm, thirty-three degrees centigrade, all determined by HAPOC. The water washed down on Viktor's body, rejuvenating him and washing him of the sweat he had accumulated while on the treadmill. He applied the shampoo that was perfect for his dense but soft hair, and he rubbed himself down with the body wash made for adding hydration to his naturally drier skin.

Droplets hit Viktor's skin and carried the undesirable bodily residues and fluids swirling down into the drain. The mess of water and filth orderly followed a path to disappear in a singular point.

Viktor was cleansed and baptized. He stepped out of the shower, dried himself with a towel, and went back into his room.

Four white walls, a square table, a sharp desk, a dresser with five drawers, and a small twin bed populated the space. It smelled of lavender, as if a flower were growing in the room itself, and natural light flooded the room through the windows. Viktor stepped toward the drawer and got dressed. He put on his underwear first. White and molded to his pelvis, it provided comfort and airflow to his genitals. He put on one white sock at a time. Then he put on his grey chino pants, tailored and tapered, and he slowly buttoned up a white collared shirt. Finally, he went back downstairs and put on his white self-lacing patent leather shoes. The monochrome outfit was complete

His body and mind were optimized both physically and chemically. With the morning routine complete, Viktor felt like a superhero who had suited up, or a battery that had just been charged. The perfect specimen had emerged from his incubation chamber and was ready for the world now. He was now ready to make his contributions to society, ready to achieve. He was ready for work.

CHAPTER III

———

Now ready for the day, Viktor stepped confidently out of his house and into the structured, organized City around him. He pulled out a handheld device that expanded into a holographic screen, made a few clicks, and used HAPOC to call an autonomous vehicle (auto), one of the thousands that were parked at equidistant stations throughout the City to save fuel and maximize availability, waiting for people to service. Soon enough, it came, and Viktor stepped in.

The drive to work was the same route as always, the fastest, most-efficient route. Enjoying the ride, Viktor glanced out of the auto and was greeted with the designed grandeur of the City. Beautiful and magnificent, white and gray towers rose up from the ground, a testament to the work and progress of society. The buildings were all high-rises, optimizing for volume and usable space. They were uniform and impeccable, spotless glass panels which both let in and reflected the dazzling sunlight. From Viktor's viewing angle, blocked by the top of the auto window, he could not see the tops of these towers.

The auto made a right turn, a truly right turn. The streets intersected at exactly ninety degrees, optimizing for turning angles in every direction. The flow of cars never stopped and there were no traffic jams—the autos had seen to that. No soiled spots could be seen on the thousands of cubic meters of glass windows. It was perfect as clockwork.

The auto arrived at Viktor's workplace, the Ministry of Progress, where all work on the HAPOC algorithm was done. As Viktor stepped out of his auto in front of the domineering Corinthian columns that marked the entrance to the ministry, he marveled at the grandeur of the building. It was built in an ancient, Greco-Roman style, but, housed within, was the technological wonder, the cutting-edge engine of society: HAPOC.

Viktor scanned his fingerprint and iris at the entrance and strolled in, walking to his desk. Despite the archaic exterior of the building, the interior was sleek and modern, equipped with state-of-the-art computer technology and designed in the style of the latest minimalistic design trends. He walked into the workspace where the employees sat and made their contributions to society.

All the scientists were already in the office. They represented a collection of different heights, ethnicities, and genders. Race and physical attributes no longer mattered here—anything could be optimized, and so long as the scientists had able minds that could contribute to the work of HAPOC, they were welcomed here.

Everyone was talking, not with each other, but with their own, personal HAPOC-enabled devices. The engineers worked in cubicles, and the floor was laid out in the manner which would enhance productivity and make work the most efficient. HAPOC made sure the engineers were allocated optimally by ability. And HAPOC told them what to do, for

HAPOC, of course, knew best how to deploy resources. It was a perfectly calculated, well-oiled machine.

Then Viktor saw his mentor, Lucius, sitting at work in his office. Lucius was middle-aged, with silver beginning to show in his hair. He was thin, much like all the other scientists who worked at the ministry. A pair of half-rimmed glasses gave him an air of erudition. He was sufficiently senior to occupy his own corner office.

Viktor and Lucius had only recently gotten to know each other, but they had quickly grown close. Though the relationship began as a mandated pairing from the Institute, now the relationship resembled that of a father and a son. Viktor respected Lucius's experience and heeded his advice and guidance, while Lucius took pleasure and felt a sense of fulfillment at seeing his mentee grow as a scientist. Lucius cared for Viktor far beyond what his duties as a mentor mandated, and Viktor had in turn come to view Lucius as a friend and confidante. Their many shared hours of programming engendered a sense of camaraderie and fellowship. Lucius tried to teach Viktor all he knew, and Viktor had had no one but Lucius when he began working at the ministry.

Viktor walked into Lucius's office and greeted him, being sure to close the door behind him. Lucius looked up from his computer but stayed seated. Upon seeing Viktor, his eyebrows perked up higher above the rims of his glasses and he smiled.

"Hey Lucius, what's to be done today?" asked Viktor, getting right to business.

Lucius smiled. "I have a special mission for you."

Viktor's ears perked up. "How can I be of service?"

"Not much work at the office, actually. In fact, you can head home as soon as I've told you your mission...." Lucius paused. "Viktor, have you heard of the Woods?"

Viktor had indeed heard of the Woods. Every person in the City knew about it. Lucius knew that, but he had asked just to see Viktor's reaction. The Woods was the vast expanse of uncivilized, wild regions that lay outside the walls of the City. Viktor and every Citizen was told that it was a place devoid of HAPOC and lay in backward squalor. Wild beasts and danger resided in the Woods.

Viktor responded, "Yes, I've heard of the Woods. We're told to never go there."

"Well you're going to be going there," said Lucius.

"What?" Viktor said, startled. His thoughts turned to beasts ripping his arms out of his body.

"It's not too bad a place, despite what they tell you. It's merely uncivilized, lacking technology. But it's not too dangerous—we just say that to keep people away because it isn't the optimal place to be. Human beings actually live there. And that's what we're interested in. Just exactly how much better is life with HAPOC than life without it? It's core to our understanding of HAPOC. And it'd be great if you could help with that. HAPOC determined you'd be a great person for the job. It's actually a great honor, you know, to be granted access to the Woods," explained Lucius. His voice, steady and persuasive, calmed Viktor's concerns.

"So, it's not really dangerous?" Viktor asked.

"No, it's just less optimal. It's less artificial, and there's less technology, maybe even none. It's still plagued by the imperfections of nature. Your job is to figure out just how imperfect," Lucius reassured Viktor.

Lucius stretched out his hand and offered Viktor a device. It was an immobilizer, a gun-shaped device that functioned like a taser. "For your protection, though I doubt you'll need it."

Viktor thought for a second and then made up his mind. He took the immobilizer from Lucius. "Then I want to do my duty. I'll take the mission. Thank you for the honor, Lucius," replied Viktor trustingly.

"Report back as soon as possible. Good luck. You're dismissed."

With that, Viktor left Lucius's office and began to walk out of the ministry the same way he came in. Now, he was alone with his thoughts. *What a quick day.* Viktor felt simultaneously honored and apprehensive at the same time. He recognized that he was receiving special treatment but was also nervous at the prospect of going into the Woods.

But Viktor knew he was strong. He had run on the treadmill daily for this. He had been optimized by HAPOC to be the best he could be and to serve the City in the best way that he could.

Viktor exited the building, walking through the Corinthian columns. He would return home and act on this later, just as the City required of him. HAPOC had selected him for this. He'd get it done.

Viktor called an auto and was dropped off back home. He also knew a silver lining awaited him—HAPOC had told him so: today was a day for romance.

CHAPTER IV

Back home from work, Viktor was excited for the afternoon, for he knew that it would be the day he found love. The algorithm was finished. He was pacing back and forth in his room, waiting for the moment. For the past few weeks, Viktor had waited anxiously for the completion of HAPOC's matchmaking algorithm. As his nerves got tighter every day, people kept telling him about their HAPOC matches. His friends at school would tell him about their HAPOC-enabled romantic excursions. He recalled a friend recounting a story about how he had met the perfect match, and Viktor could still remember the star-struck gleam in his friend's eyes as he described the encounter.

Viktor hadn't needed to do anything. HAPOC already knew what he liked and what would be a good match. After all, it saw everything. For his entire life, HAPOC had been documenting everything in order to deliver Viktor an optimal life. It took into account every conversation he had, other's thoughts about him, his school records, his genetics, his physical features, and much, much more. Such was the case for everyone in the City.

As Viktor was sitting on the bed, the moment came. Surrounded by the familiar four white walls of his bedroom, a buzz on his phone jolted him to attention. He'd been overexcited about every notification for the past hour, like a dog jumping at a hand waving a tennis ball. This time, it was real. The screen read, "Alice Locke. Age: Nineteen. Proceed to meeting point at the Egg Café. Wear red. Please take AMOUR pill before arrival at Egg Café." A picture of Alice flashed on the screen. Red hair, freckles, capped off with a charming smile—Viktor was immediately entranced. He stared at the picture, unable to avert his eyes. His lips slowly curled up into a smile as he thought of her and their potential future together. Viktor was completely enamored. He had no reason not to be—after all, HAPOC had optimized according to his preferences.

"Alice," he whispered softly to himself.

Viktor kept her image in his mind and the smile on his face as he sprang into action. Picking out a red button-down shirt, he proceeded to put it on. He ran to the bathroom and checked his reflection in the mirror. Turning on the tap, Viktor wetted his hand and then ran it through his hair to quickly style it.

HAPOC buzzed. "Apply styling gel," a mechanical voice said, evidently unsatisfied with Viktor's lazy attempt at fixing his hair. Viktor followed orders, opening a jar of hair gel and dipping his finger in. In his nervous haste, Viktor took out way too much gel, and dipped his finger back into the jar to put some back. He applied it to his hair, and it became glossy and layered.

"Apply cologne," said HAPOC, sensing the less-than-great smells coming from Viktor.

Following orders again, Viktor reached for his cologne. He gave himself a puff on the neck. But he aimed too high. Eau de parfum went up his nose and mouth, and Viktor went into a coughing fit. One cough. Two. Three. Ten. Finally, Viktor settled down. He paused, looked in the mirror, and smelled himself. His cologne smelled great.

Exasperated at all the commands and seeking to bolt out the door to see Alice as soon as possible, Viktor said, knowing HAPOC would hear him, "Anything else?"

"Take AMOUR pill," reminded HAPOC.

The Attraction and Mating Optimization and Upgrading Resource (AMOUR) pill was a scientific breakthrough. It made a user more flirtatious and fostered the secretion of more pheromones. It decreased inhibitions and allowed for greater connection with other pill users. In short, it made one perfectly ready for a date. Viktor opened the glass bottle of AMOUR pills, popping one of the red capsules into his mouth. He sunk his teeth into it, and a syrupy-sweet liquid seeped out onto his tongue, which he swallowed quickly.

Now all ready, Viktor left the bathroom and ran down the stairs to make his way to the Egg Café, which was five minutes from his home and a favorite destination of Viktor. Three quarters of the way down the stairs, Viktor stumbled, losing his footing and falling down the final three steps onto the first floor.

"Take it slower," chided HAPOC. Viktor felt more humiliation than physical pain. "One step at a time. Put on your shoes and get to the rendezvous point," continued HAPOC.

Viktor put on his shoes and stepped out of his house. He called an auto. Soon enough, it came, a white streak on the black pavement that slowed to a halt in front of him. Viktor stepped into the auto and got comfortable on the leather seats, kept cool by the A/C that monitored the passenger's vital signs to ensure that the temperature was optimal. The drive lasted five minutes, and Viktor spent those five minutes thinking about Alice. The drive was smooth, and the auto made no sound save for a faint electrical humming, leaving Viktor at peace with his thoughts of Alice. Through the tinted windows, everything he saw reminded him of her visage, which he had only seen virtually. His expectations were higher than the skyscrapers outside, and every red made him think of her red hair. Soon enough, he arrived at the Café, and it was time to meet her.

CHAPTER V

———

Viktor entered the café. The setting was familiar, as Viktor had come to the Egg Café many times. The walls were white, with painted yellow circles dotting the wallpaper, evoking the image of yellow yolk surrounded by egg white. The smell of fried and scrambled eggs wafted through the air. It smelled like the morning, like the aroma that wafted through open air cafés in centuries past. Tables and booths filled the interior, all painted white and yellow. Viktor scanned the restaurant and glimpsed a streak of red—it was Alice, already sitting at a booth.

They made eye contact with each other, and then Alice broke into a beautiful smile. Her lips curled up at the edges, and lines appeared at the corners of her eyes, signaling the authenticity of the smile. In that moment, upon seeing that smile, Viktor was at ease, now feeling comfortable and welcomed, as he approached this new person for the first time. He made his way over.

"What took you so long, Viktor?" Alice playfully asked, opening the conversation. Her voice sounded like chiming bells, clear, melodious, and resonant.

"It's my first time with HAPOC Match. You're Alice, right?" replied Viktor nervously.

"Of course I am. Why else would I be here and how else would I know your name, you dummy?" Her blue eyes sparkled as she teased Viktor sarcastically. "Take a seat," Alice chirped. She scooted over on the cushion of the booth, making room for him beside her. She was close enough for Viktor to smell the redolent fragrance that emanated from her person. It smelled subtle and pleasant, like sheets fresh out of the dryer.

Viktor was caught off guard by Alice's strong but fun first impression, how assertive she was, how her flair complemented her fiery and beautiful appearance perfectly, and how she called him "dummy."

He felt his cheeks redden a bit, and, as he looked at her, he reoriented himself. *Just be confident. It's going to be a good time. This is already optimized for you.*

Instead of sitting next to Alice, Viktor sat down across from her. "Haha, you're right ... Well, I'm Viktor and I'm pleased to meet you. Have you been here before? I've been a thousand times. I live a five-minute auto ride away."

"A thousand times? You must be obsessed with eggs. I've never been here, but I absolutely love eggs. How do you like yours?" Alice asked.

Indeed, Viktor loved eggs. He had been frequenting the Egg Cafe for many years now, cultivating his appreciation for eggs. Eggs were a staple of life in the City. HAPOC and the City had identified them as an intensely protein-rich food, and gene-editing technology had enabled scientists to remove the high cholesterol content from them. HAPOC made sure eggs were a part of everyone's diet. And for Viktor, HAPOC had determined the best type of egg for his digestion and tastes—but Viktor had extrapolated his own sense of meaning from HAPOC's determination.

Viktor replied, "I prefer them fried, with a slightly runny yolk. It's really an art, to get that result. And the idea of a delicious core being held precariously within a fragile exterior that can be so easily broken appeals to me. One wrong move of the fork and the treasure will spill out, ruined, almost wasted. It's a worthwhile challenge to maintain the perfection of the egg and to capture all the yolk in your mouth without wasting a single drop. I love—"

Alice loudly giggled, leading to redness filling Viktor's cheeks. He watched her laugh, seeing the mouth open in an expression of joy. Her pearly whites stared back at him. The jovial sound that came out was music to his ears.

"You're so funny. Do you start all your dates with streams of consciousness about eggs? I love how unfiltered and quirky you are. And how philosophical and meaningful you can make an egg sound. And I totally feel the same way. Fried with a runny yolk is my egg of choice as well, and HAPOC tells me it's the right type for me, though I had never reflected so deeply on why it's so appealing, as you seem to have."

Viktor was bursting with joy on the inside. Someone who genuinely found his nerdy and quirky demeanor interesting and shared the same weird esoteric preference that he did. To Viktor, Alice's voice felt like a rhythmic, melodious flow of sound waves. What were the odds? Viktor knew whom he had to thank—HAPOC. Of course, it paired him with someone who had the same food preferences. Such was the genius of HAPOC.

Realizing how giddy he must have looked at that moment, Viktor slowly took a sip of water to settle himself down. The

L-theanine infused in the water made sure that Viktor, indeed, was calmed down.

"Alice, wow, I've never met anyone who appreciated my weird views about eggs like you. HAPOC is really outdoing itself with this one," Viktor chuckled in reply.

"Yeah, can you imagine how tedious meeting people would be before HAPOC was around? Like, how did our grandparents even live?" mused Alice. "By the way, why don't we order those eggs already?"

Both ordered two eggs each, sunny side up. Of course, regardless of the exterior appearance, each egg was optimized for its eater. Personal preferences, genetic specifications, and more were given as inputs to HAPOC, who made sure that all food was customized to be optimal in taste and nutrition. HAPOC's outputs would then be sent to the machines that acted as the chefs and food producers of the City. After all, automation was more efficient. The entire food supply chain was managed mostly by automatons, who prepared and cooked food to be consumed by citizens.

The eggs came, and they ate them delicately, being careful not to spill the yolk too much.

In between bites, Viktor came back to Alice's question, "Our grandparents must have lived miserable lives, never knowing what to do, being ensnared by uncertainty."

"You're so right. I've enjoyed this meal so very much, and that was never in question, because HAPOC is always right."

"I heard people used to aimlessly 'date,' trying their luck on meeting people over and over again until they found someone they were satisfied with. Sounds awful."

"Exactly. Now, we all get our 'ones' on the first try. I don't want to be too forward, but just to state a fact, it's so great that HAPOC knows from the get-go that we share the most in common and would enjoy each other's company very much, as we have. Not to mention that HAPOC knows we'd probably have the optimal offspring, given our compatible genetics," Alice intimated.

Viktor burped awkwardly and he blushed at Alice's suggestion. Recomposing himself, he continued the line of thought, "HAPOC is indeed an infinitely better decision maker than our feeble human minds. Perfecting HAPOC's algorithm is actually what I do for work. Making sure it's as accurate as can be."

"Viktor, that's awesome! You're actually a programmer of the System!"

Viktor hesitated on what to say next. An idea had come to him. *Why don't I invite Alice on my mission? We'd get to spend more time together and maybe she'll be impressed with me. But it's risky. What if she doesn't like the idea?* He looked at Alice and saw a welcoming smile. Reassured by her open body language, Viktor decided to give the idea a try. Maybe he'd let her in on his mission.

"Yeah, it's great. Now that you mention it, they've actually been wanting me to do a kind of personal test of the system. To see precisely how much of an improvement HAPOC is on our lives, they told me to act independently of HAPOC and see how my experiences compare. Maybe we could try it out together?" Viktor continued. He voiced the question meekly, unsure how Alice would receive such an idea.

Alice blinked a few times. Viktor waited for her reaction, nervously. Then she smiled even wider. Alice was intrigued. She leaned in closer to Viktor as the notion moved her to the edge of her seat. "What an adventurous idea! I've never thought about that, acting without HAPOC. I'm not sure what I would do."

Viktor was relieved by her apparent interest. He grew more emboldened, his voice rising a bit in volume. "Well, there's only one way to find out, and I want to find out with you!"

"That sounds exciting, what do you have in mind?" asked Alice.

This next part was going to be the hardest to ask. But Viktor mustered up the courage and asked anyway. "Have you ever been to the Woods?"

Alice was taken aback by the suggestion. "The Woods? Isn't that where the suboptimal people go?" her eyes grew wide.

"Exactly, which would make it the perfect place for our little experiment."

"Isn't it dangerous? I've heard that it's not a place for people like us. Will we even be allowed to leave the City?"

Alice had heard the same stories about the Woods that Viktor had. She knew it as a place best avoided, full of mystery and danger.

"Don't worry; I have authorization—my work is supervised directly by the Overseer of our City. You can come along as my assistant," Viktor affirmed. He puffed out his chest in a show of confidence.

"Have you been there before?" inquired Alice.

"No, this assignment was just handed to me very recently. I've heard about the Woods and been briefed on it, of course. Supposedly, it's a place beset by the ravages of nature, without the benefits of any of our technological advancements such as HAPOC."

"The people there must live terrible lives then. Are you sure going there's a good idea?" asked Alice warily.

"Yep, that's the assumption, but we need to know for sure. Let's see how we do living like them, without the assistance of HAPOC."

In his mind, Viktor imagined people living like the cave dwellers he had read about in his history classes—men and women covered in scraps of animal hide, foraging to survive and at the mercy of nature with no technological protections anywhere. The quality of life seemed so base, so crude.

"What about the dangerous suboptimal people?"

"We'll be safe, don't worry. They wouldn't let any harm come to a HAPOC engineer. They gave me an immobilizer, look." Viktor pulled out of his pocket the small gun-shaped device. Holding it made him feel empowered, stronger.

"What does it do?"

"If anything dangerous comes our way, I just point at it and press this trigger, and the threat will be immobilized. Don't worry."

"That's reassuring. How do we get there?"

Viktor smiled as he flashed his badge. "I know the way; it's right outside the Southern Gate. There will, of course, be guards protecting our border and regulating inflow and outflow of people, but just stay with me, and we'll make it through."

"Okay, I'll trust you on this one, but if we suffer horrible fates, I'm putting the blame on you," teased Alice. She chuckled and her quiet laughter filled Viktor's ears.

The two finished their meals and exited the Cafe. The day was sunny with few clouds in the sky. The sun was dropping down from its zenith.

Sensing that they had walked out and had both been exhibiting high levels of chemicals associated with positive emotion, HAPOC chimed in again in a unified voice, a combination of the version customized for Viktor and the one that was customized for Alice, "That was a great date! Want to do it again?"

A little annoyed at HAPOC for interrupting the moment, Viktor replied, "Thanks for your help, HAPOC." Then he turned to Alice and suggested, "Let's get going to the Woods, then."

Alice looked worried. Her eyebrows furrowed as she thought about the implications.

"Wouldn't using your badge and telling the guards that I'm your assistant be lying? And isn't lying suboptimal?" questioned Alice.

"It's just a little lie; don't worry. And after all, it's for the good of everyone. HAPOC wants it. This is an official mission from the government," replied Viktor.

"But I thought we were told never to lie," said Alice

"Don't think about it as a lie. Think about it as just carrying out the orders of our government. Besides, you'll be helping me. So, you're my assistant," said Viktor. He struggled to reassure Alice. He moved closer to her and put his hand on her arm. The touching of skin caused endorphins to rush through his mind.

"But that's not what it is. The orders of the government are for you to go out into the Woods. Nothing was ever said about me. I'm not your assistant."

"Trust me; I have discretionary authority over the particulars of my mission. And besides, you would be helping the end goal of the government in this mission. A small inaccuracy in your position or title actually isn't so bad, especially if, in the end, it's in service of our society," replied Viktor.

"I don't know about this, Viktor. This all makes me feel so … suboptimal. In fact, I've never felt this suboptimal before," said Alice.

"I'm trying to reach the optimal outcome here. Don't you think it would be optimal for our happiness? Why else would HAPOC match us together? And together, we can make greater contributions to HAPOC in this mission."

"Viktor, you're putting your personal desires above the rules of our society."

"HAPOC was made to serve our desires, to make us have the happiest lives. I would know; I work on it," retorted Viktor. Switching to a more tender tone, he continued, "Alice, this day has been a blast. I only ask that you trust me on this one. I promise it'll be fun. And you have my word, as a government employee, that neither you nor I are suboptimal. Is that okay with you?"

Alice paused for a beat. She looked Viktor in the eye. The AMOUR pill's effects still pushed her to want to be with Viktor.

"Promise me we'll be okay," she said.

"I promise." Viktor smiled at Alice, and her lips slowly curled up and returned the smile as she gazed into Viktor's now contented face.

"Okay. And what would I be doing as your 'assistant'?"

"Just be with me. Be alert to what's around us, especially to anything you find unusual. Keep mental notes. But, most importantly, let's spend some fun and exciting times together!" replied Viktor, now very upbeat.

"Sounds good, let's do it then."

"I'll call an auto. Thanks for coming with me, Alice."

Acting on his words, Viktor called an auto with the destination set for the Southern Gate. An empty red auto stopped by the road and the two hopped in.

Inside the vehicle, they sat together. Though the back of the vehicle had three seats, Alice had chosen the middle seat to be closer to Viktor. And whether it was due to the influence of AMOUR pills or something else, Alice began to lean ever so slightly on Viktor.

Viktor, simultaneously excited yet addled by this development, felt his body tingle. He didn't know what to do.

At that moment, a mechanical voice sounded on the vehicle's speakers. "Put your arm around her. Pheromone levels are appropriate," said HAPOC. So, Viktor willed his arm around Alice's shoulder.

Alice laughed, "That's better. Bet you couldn't have done that on your own."

"Well, HAPOC was invented for a reason, might as well use it. Now we have this nice moment because of it," Viktor said in defense.

"Glad we have good old HAPOC. By the way, what exactly is it that you work on for HAPOC?" asked Alice.

"I work on the algorithm. Making sure that the outputs of HAPOC are as optimal as can be. Making sure that it accounts for all possibilities and contexts, so that it can truly give us the perfect outcome. I know it's weird to think of HAPOC as being imperfect and needing improvement, but after all, it was designed by humans. And don't worry, we're pretty darn close to perfection," Viktor replied, beaming with pride.

As the auto zoomed through the streets of the City, Viktor glanced outside the auto window. Monumental silvery towers filled the view, and from the auto Viktor could only see a small fraction of the true size of the skyscrapers.

"Wow, so you're the guy making the world a better, more optimal place," said Alice.

"Haha, I guess you could say that. It's really fulfilling, knowing that my work can make everyone else's lives better."

"What's HAPOC like?"

"HAPOC's a big guy. He occupies a room in our facility, from which he can communicate to all the other millions of HAPOC-enabled devices in the world, like this car—it gets signals from the room. The interesting thing is that there's really not much to see. The awesome power of HAPOC is just some computers and wires hooked up together that use the right few lines of code—well, not a few, thousands and thousands and thousands."

Viktor beamed as he explained. Alice's questioning gave him an excuse to show off the work he took so much pride in, and her curiosity served to validate his belief that he was indeed playing an instrumental part in making the world a better place.

"So, a bunch of wires are responsible for all of this," Alice remarked as she gestured by moving her hands outwards.

"A bunch of wires and our code, that is."

"And how did you land such a cool gig?"

"Well, the government came to our school and administered a test, and I performed the best on it. So, they interviewed me and decided I was fit for the job. HAPOC decided I was as well. And I mean, I was also meant for it. HAPOC already knows what we like and what the optimal job would be for us. I'm sure it was the same for you. It's the optimal job for me."

"And where'd you go to school?" asked Alice.

"I went to the Engineering School of our City," said Viktor. "It's an awesome place. We all enjoyed it. Well, that's to be expected. After all, HAPOC selected that school as the one that best suits our abilities and preferences. How about you?"

"I went to the Art School. Always wanted to be a sketch artist. Loved the way that small, gray scratches of a pencil on paper can combine to form such beautiful sketches. And HAPOC recognized that. HAPOC knew from the start. So, it put me in the Art School, and I love it," replied Alice.

"Then you must like the scenery outside. All those sharp angles, perfectly perpendicular streets, just like a blueprint," said Viktor.

"Yeah, it's perfect. We get everything down to the T. We can build it in real life even better than I can draw it on paper. Every angle is always ninety degrees. Never a degree more or less. Makes the roads run better. Turning is easiest when intersections are at ninety degrees," Alice remarked as the auto made a turn, as if it were listening to the conversation.

"Yeah, it's sharp. No inefficiencies. Our city is a perfect grid. No space wasted. No confusion," Viktor continued. "What do you like to draw?"

"Cubes. Perfectly shaped. Equal in every dimension, length, width, and height. Just trying to reproduce the perfection of our world on paper. Difference is, our world is HAPOC-powered, whereas my sketches are powered by my own fingers," said Alice.

"That's a great way to put it," replied Viktor.

"How did everything work before HAPOC? I've always been curious—I mean, beyond what the government says—and it sounds like you'd know a thing or two," continued Alice.

"It's pretty in-line with what the government says, to my knowledge. Seems like life was nasty, brutish, and short. All the things that could go wrong would go wrong. What else would you expect with no HAPOC to correct for suboptimality? And it's good that you're curious. This trip will be perfect for us to find out with our own eyes," said Viktor.

And with that, the vehicle stopped and HAPOC spoke, "Destination reached. Please collect belongings and exit the vehicle."

Viktor and Alice stepped out, and the auto drove itself away. In front of them was a massive wall, at least a hundred feet high. It curved toward the edges of their ranges of vision, for the wall encircled the City. It curved perfectly and shone with the same bright silvery color that characterized the structures of the City. Near the level of the ground was a gate, operated by a few soldiers.

"Follow me," said Viktor.

They walked along the granite path that led to the gate, and with each step Viktor and Alice readied themselves to speak with the guards and ensure their safe passage. But that proved to be unnecessary.

As they came to the front of the gate, the soldiers seemed not to notice them, standing perfectly on guard, immovable like statues.

Then, HAPOC's voice chimed in, "System Engineer Zero-One-Three. You are cleared for exit."

Now, the soldiers moved. One of them pushed a button, and a large gate opened, revealing a patch of greenery.

They exited the City through the gate and went into the field.

CHAPTER VI

As they passed through the gate, HAPOC went offline.

"We're on our own now. Let's make the most of it," said Viktor.

"I trust you," replied Alice uncertainly. She clutched onto Viktor's arm as they came into the Woods.

An idyllic scene awaited Viktor and Alice. Beyond the gray, high, bland walls that encircled the City was a pastoral field of greenery. They were on a dirt path that cut through a small, flat, green field. The path stretched from the Gate, across the expanse of the field, and then into a wooded area far off in the distance.

"Guess that area with the trees over there is the Woods," said Viktor.

He took Alice's hand and they made their way across the field. With each step, the tree line grew closer and closer, and soon they crossed it.

They entered now into a natural place with more vegetation than either had seen in their entire lives within the confines of their artificial fortress of the City. It had long been the belief of the Council of Overseers that governed society that nature was imperfect and that a better, synthetic world could be created to rectify the errors of nature. To that end, they had created a society of artificial optimality, removing the discomforts of nature, and replacing them with streamlined manufactured efficiency.

But now, trees were everywhere; sunlight broke through the canopy and rays shone onto the ground. The light was golden as amber. Verdant green leaves growing on brown branches filled the space. The ground underneath them was darker than it had been on the path closer to the Gate. Flowers of red, orange, violet, and blue bloomed around them.

"How ... lush," Viktor said as he searched for an adequate descriptor.

"It's so bright. I've never seen so much color in one place before," added Alice.

The different wavelengths of the colors of nature flooded the rods and cones of the young couple's eyes, and they took a minute to adjust to the new environment. Alice brushed her hair behind her ears to keep it from being scattered by the breeze. Viktor looked up into the sky and watched a bird overhead. He stopped to touch a leaf on a tree. It felt smooth yet coarse. Curious at the rare natural object, Viktor pressed his fingers on it, breaking the leaf by accident, leading to a minuscule amount of plant fluid staining his hands.

"This is nothing like home. It's so wild and natural. It feels so brutish and crude, yet there's a certain beauty to it. I guess, so far, we're doing alright without HAPOC," Viktor mused.

"You're right, it could even be quite lovely if I didn't know how deprived the people who must live here are. Speaking of the people, where are they?"

"There." Viktor pointed to a clearing in the distance. A faint plume of smoke was rising up into the sky.

"But there's no road. How are we going to get there?" asked Alice, still unfamiliar with the pastoral scene. "We can still move our legs, regardless of whether there's a road or not. Let's go."

They walked toward the sign of civilization.

As they approached the clearing, they began to hear the familiar sounds of human civilization, but they also heard the unfamiliar sounds of nature. Birds chirped in the distance. The leaves rustled as small rodents scurried across the ground. A squirrel darted across the path. Though they knew it was harmless, the pure novelty of such a thing caused Alice to leap back in fear. A deer pranced across in front of them and stopped for a second, looking at Alice and Viktor with curiosity, before prancing back into the wild.

"All these wild animals. I thought we had gotten rid of all of them. I've only seen them in my history books. They won't hurt us, right?' asked Alice.

"No, I remember reading that that big one with antlers is called a 'deer.' It only ate plants and wasn't aggressive to humans. Let's just get to the clearing. It looks like there's a settlement of some sort there," Viktor replied.

"Did you see the antlers on that deer? Some of it was broken off. And it had scars on its body. The poor thing. The Woods seems so dangerous. No one in the City gets hurt like that," remarked Alice.

"Really makes you appreciate HAPOC even more, doesn't it?" said Viktor.

They walked on, and on both sides of their trail Alice and Viktor noticed things they had never seen before. They saw wilted plants and a few trees that had fallen over. Viktor took a step forward and landed on a branch, hearing a crack.

"You know, there's a beautiful air to all of this, but look at all the imperfections. Within this great lively forest, so many things look like they're dying, diseased, or hurt. Guess that's what happens when no one's there to keep everything alive and healthy," observed Viktor.

"You're so right. We're definitely getting some good results for that mission of yours. My verdict on HAPOC is that it's really done wonders. Look at all the bad things that are happening in its absence," Alice responded.

They continued, until suddenly Viktor's foot caught itself in a root on the ground, causing him to trip. But he was holding Alice's hand, which kept him safe. He instinctively squeezed her hand tighter and used it to steady himself. Though she lurched forward a little, the added leverage helped Viktor regain his balance and avoided a fall onto sharp rocks.

"Are you alright?" asked Alice, startled by the sudden shift in momentum.

Viktor's heart raced. A surge of adrenaline had pulsed through his body as he tripped. Though no harm had come to him, he still felt fear. Small beads of sweat appeared on his forehead.

"That was scary, Alice. Something really bad almost happened to me just now. This place, for all its beauty, is dangerous. We have to remember that. I'm sorry for almost making you fall too," Viktor replied.

In that moment of danger, Alice's heartbeat had quickened as well. They stopped in their paths, turned, and locked eyes. He focused on her deep blue irises. Alice's red hair reflected onto her eyes, giving them a tender amber undertone. They felt pulses of romance course through their bodies, stimulated by the adrenaline rush. They drew closer to each other and Viktor took Alice by both hands.

"It's okay; neither of us were hurt. It was so frightening in the moment, and my heart's still racing, but I'm with you, and this makes me feel so … alive," replied Alice. Viktor could see that her pupils were dilated. A few strands of her rufescent hair lay on the side of her face, blown there by the gentle breeze. They rested like autumn leaves on a bed of grass, dyed red by the changing of the seasons.

They were reoriented now, no longer in danger, but their hearts still raced.

Viktor ran a nervous hand through his hair. "It's still dawning on me how easily we could have ended up seriously hurt." He looked around him and continued. "There's so much uncertainty and surprise here. Anything out here can hurt you. Really makes you feel your own mortality. We're such delicate creatures—that's why we need HAPOC. Otherwise we'll break so easily," Viktor mused.

Alice responded to his thoughtful words. "That rush though—I know you felt it too. I don't think it could have happened without the danger. What is this we're feeling now? It feels so lovely. I feel so light."

Viktor felt it too. The tingling feeling in his skin. The butterflies in his stomach. The rush that the danger brought had awoken something within him. He was mortal, and he had better make the most of his life. Every inch of him felt like lunging forward and embracing the sweet-smelling, beautiful lady who stood in front of him with her hands in his. Her words made him feel that the moment was right.

Pushed to action by this newfound feeling, Viktor continued, "Alice …"

He stared at her for a moment, then he moved forward. Tilting his head slowly to the right, he angled his head forward and touched his lips to hers, just like in the old movies he had watched in the City. Their eyes both closed, and he felt her exerting force back onto his lips. His arms came around her body and embraced her. Viktor felt her hands on his back too, and for a few moments that felt frozen in time, they shared an ethereal kiss.

In the middle of a forest, with sunlight breaking through the trees, two figures merged into one. The sun shone on this incongruous couple dressed in synthetic garb standing in the middle of nature, kissing under an old, primeval tree whose branches sheltered them like arms on a giant.

Finally, they released each other.

"That was amazing, Alice," sighed Viktor.

"Yeah, why do I have a feeling that that wouldn't have happened in the City?" replied Alice.

"I'm not sure." He took hold of her hand again. "Let's keep going; maybe there are more beautiful things to discover."

They held hands and continued down the idyllic path that lead them deeper into the dangerous Woods, smiling softly at each other as they walked.

CHAPTER VII

———

With their hearts content, Viktor and Alice kept walking. They looked at each other tenderly and frequently while they played with each other's hands. He would rub his thumb on her hand, and she would return the favor, both unable to get enough of the other's touch. In this state, they walked further and further into the Woods.

Eventually, they reached a clearing. The trees thinned out and the view forward was now unobstructed by trees and foliage. In front of them, a settlement awaited.

There, they looked upon houses made of wood, people dressed in ragged clothes leading farm animals, and the stench of bodies and animals in the air—far cries from the modern comforts afforded to them in the City. Both humans and animals walked on the dirt paths. Trees dotted the sides of the paths in the spaces between the houses. The leaves and branches swayed with the wind. The settlement was painted in greens and browns and yellows, with the occasional white and pink from cows and pigs entering the frame. It looked quintessentially bucolic. Unlike in the City, the people moved almost lazily, seemingly unhurried and unconcerned with efficiency. A young man was chopping wood in a yard. A woman was milking a cow. Another was knitting on a chair. Children were running around, frolicking in the streets.

A voice shouted, "Looks like we have visitors from the City!" Many men and women of the village looked up and their gaze fell upon Viktor and Alice. The murmuring was audible.

An elderly yet strong-looking man approached. He was clean-shaven, though wrinkled with age. His hair was dashed with silver streaks, and on his face, he carried an avuncular smile. He was tall and well-built for a man his age. His arms were twice the size of Viktor's, despite his age. He had been sitting on a porch in the same yard as the man chopping wood and had gotten up when the commotion started. He slowly walked up to where Alice and Viktor stood on the dirt path.

"Hello, my name is Hugo." He offered out a handshake. "You must be from the City. A rare treat. Welcome to the Woods."

Viktor stepped forward and took the handshake. "I'm Victor, and this is Alice. We indeed are from the City."

Seeing that Hugo had gone ahead to deal with the visitors, the crowd returned to their business.

Hugo smiled. "Of course, you might need some time to adjust. You may find our quaint, green sanctuary a bit antiquated, but we all were once like you as well, living in the City."

"Yes, what exactly is all this? Like those animals, I've never seen them before, though I've read about them," said Viktor.

"Why, this is our humble village. We live, work, and play here just as you do in the City. These are our homes, and those are cows and pigs and chickens. Animals we raise for companionship and sustenance. I'm sure you've had a steak before. This is what the steak looks like when it's alive," replied Hugo, pointing at a cow teasingly.

"You said you used to live in the City?" Alice asked.

"Why yes, but we find it much better here in the Woods without the burdens of your technology. We live simple and humble lives, but we're happy, even if we lack the hedonistic comforts of yours," replied Hugo.

"What do you mean?" asked Viktor, curious at Hugo's assertion.

"Look around you. None of us make use of your fancy HAPOC system. We simply live according to our own needs and wants. Which makes me wonder, how did you two come to be together? The classic HAPOC-arranged meeting, was it not?" challenged Hugo.

"Well, you're right that HAPOC brought us together. That's something we're thankful to HAPOC for," replied Viktor.

"So young, so naïve. You two must be tired. Come with me. We can rest in my home." Hugo motioned for Alice and Viktor to follow him. He walked toward the yard with the young man chopping wood. Alice and Viktor followed.

As they entered the yard with the man chopping wood, Hugo stopped and yelled at the man, "Jurgen, we have guests!" With one final swing of the axe, the man stopped, lodged the axe into a nearby tree stump, setting it at rest, and then came to the three. He looked like a younger version of Hugo, having the same facial structure, albeit with fewer wrinkles. Jurgen had grown a beard and had a rugged appearance to him. He was tall and bulky, and those traits translated well to chopping wood. The man was sweating and his muscles were flexed. They were massive. Viktor had never seen someone so large, muscles so meaty, or sweat so profuse. After all, they had no need for muscles and sweating in the City.

Hugo turned to Alice and Viktor and said, "This is my son, Jurgen." And then to Jurgen, "Here we have Alice and Viktor, visitors from the City. Let's go inside. Jurgen, thank you for preparing the wood."

The four made their way into Hugo's home, a structure built from many slabs of wood, pieced together with the manual labor of father and son. The walls were drab and brown, the same as the color of the wood. A rustic feel accompanied the room. Unlit candles and sconces lay around in the room, but for now, sunlight flowed in through a window and illuminated the interior. To Viktor, it felt like poverty. Poor in taste, poor in living standards, and poor in comfort. They had no perfect angles or minimalistic designs as they had in the City. A circular wooden table awaited them, and they each took seats around the table.

"So, what brings you here?" asked Hugo.

"This is his idea of a date," replied Alice, retaining her cheery, teasing nature amidst the new, bewildering environment.

"We're here to experience life without HAPOC. It's part work, part romance, actually," added Viktor.

"Interesting, and what do you do for work?" continued Hugo.

"I work on the HAPOC algorithm. You said you lived in the City once. How did you come to be here?" Viktor responded.

Hugo bristled. His muscles tensed. His eyebrows furrowed. "Ah, the inevitable question. Let's just say that I wanted to find a better way to live, and I did. But you, you align yourself with HAPOC. You dedicate your efforts toward it. Why?"

Alice replied for Viktor, "He's helping to make life better for everyone. To make sure everyone has an optimal time while alive." She smiled with pride.

Viktor countered, "What do you know about HAPOC?"

Hugo smirked, "Just that it's not the best thing for us humans, despite its insistence on optimality."

Viktor grew belligerent as he saw this old man question his work. "What do you mean?"

"I assure you that we live better here," said Hugo.

Alice looked at Hugo with skepticism. "You say this is a better way to live. In what way?"

"This is a natural place, where we can live as we were meant to live. As humans with our own choices. I'm happy. I'm in a community that values freedom," said Hugo with an air of pride.

"But your life seems so … suboptimal. Our City could probably match the annual production of your village in a single day. Where are all the machines? It looks like everyone is doing so much unnecessary, laborious work," retorted Viktor. He and Alice exchanged glances.

"Unnecessary and laborious, you say. But I see value in adversity. More importantly, I see value in freedom. Jurgen chooses to chop wood in his way, just as I chose to build this house and live my life this way. So, let me ask you one question: When was the last time, before you came today to the Woods, that you made a significant decision for yourself, not relying on HAPOC?" challenged Hugo.

Alice and Viktor stared silently at Hugo, both struggling to find an adequate answer. An awkward and long moment of silence followed.

Hugo continued. "Exactly, you can't think of one. That's because every move you make isn't your own. From the moment you wake up every day to the person you will marry, it's all preordained by whatever HAPOC tells you. And every instance of your life is devoid of adversity, devoid of true fulfillment. You pop a pill when unhappy and take supplements to solve your problems."

"But our lives are so great. Viktor and I just met today yet I can't help but feel like I've found my one in a million match," replied Alice.

"Just AMOUR pills at work. You didn't even choose each other. HAPOC made you meet. Your whole romance is artificially manufactured. Just another shortcut. In your City, nothing is earned, so nothing is meaningful. But never mind. You wouldn't understand without experiencing it. You have much to learn." Hugo turned to Jurgen. "Jurgen, why don't you take Viktor with you and teach him how to chop wood. Alice, my wife Sophia will be home very soon, why don't you sew with her when she comes? It's time for you each to earn something."

Alice and Viktor looked at each other, both shocked at the harshness of Hugo's words. Then, Jurgen spoke.

"Come along, Viktor. Let's go into the yard."

Viktor was curious. This was something new, something that could really help him collect some good data for his mission. But this also sounded like an order. Perhaps a life of unquestioningly following directives from HAPOC made him instinctively want to obey the command. In any case, Viktor got up and followed Jurgen into the yard.

CHAPTER VIII

———

Jurgen and Viktor went back out to the yard again to chop wood, while Alice waited in the house with Hugo for his wife Sophia to come home so they could knit.

Viktor was still puzzled over his inability to answer Hugo's question. *When was the last time he ever made a significant decision purely by himself? Had his life indeed been dictated by HAPOC the whole time, as Hugo had said? But even if that were true, why would that be such a bad thing?*

"Viktor, I know my father can be ... forceful at times, but I hope you have a good time with us in the Woods. I will teach you how to chop wood," said Jurgen as the two entered the yard.

The yard was messy. Jurgen's axe was at its resting place, the blade digging into a stump. Near it was a pile of chopped logs that Jurgen had finished, and on the opposite side was a pile of wood that had yet to be chopped. It smelled of fresh shrubbery and dirt.

"Thank you for your hospitality. May I ask why your father left the City? I still don't seem to understand," replied Viktor.

"Here, take the axe. We can talk about my father while we chop," said Jurgen.

"But I don't know anything about chopping," said Viktor. He eyed the axe with unease. A fearsome tool used for backbreaking, dangerous labor—Viktor felt totally out of his element. He looked around, expecting for HAPOC to show up and help him perform the task and handle the tool. But nothing came.

"I'll show you, just take the axe in your hand for now."

Viktor stepped up to the stump, and then pulled the axe out with some difficulty. It felt heavy in his hand. The steel was sharp, and the handle smooth. The wood felt like it once belonged to a tree.

"How does it feel?" asked Jurgen.

"Heavy … but ergonomic," replied Viktor.

"Now give it to me and watch," said Jurgen.

Viktor handed him the axe. Jurgen took it. He then grabbed a log, placing it on a stump that acted as a chopping block. He placed his right foot in front of his left, ready to strike. Then, in an exaggerated motion, he brought the axe up, behind his back, and then down again into the log, splitting it perfectly in two.

Viktor looked on with awe. Never before had he seen someone do such a thing. It was the greatest feat of strength he had ever laid eyes upon. He felt a sense of admiration for Jurgen, the uncivilized brute.

"Now you try. Just do as I did," said Jurgen. He handed the axe to Viktor and then placed another log onto the block.

Viktor took the axe and walked up to the block apprehensively. It was a very heavy weight for the white-collar man who had spent years sitting in an office and his hour of daily exercise on an indoor treadmill. He felt his small muscles strain under the weight. But watching Jurgen chop the wood perfectly had inspired within Viktor a small sense of jealousy and insecurity. He wanted to show Jurgen that he could easily replicate the feat, though he knew that there was a good chance that he couldn't. Compared to the brawny, strong, and manly Jurgen, Viktor felt a little emasculated.

He stood by the block and planted his feet. In an exertion of energy, Viktor brought the axe up, behind his back, and then down again. Boom.

He missed the log completely, digging the axe into the stump. He stumbled as the axe and his body's momentum dragged him forward. Viktor looked up at Jurgen, a bit embarrassed.

"Good swing; just focus on the log with your eyes," said Jurgen.

"If I chop it, will you tell me about your father?" asked Viktor.

"Yes."

With that reassurance, Viktor lifted the axe once more, brought it up above his head, and swung down. The axe slammed into the log at a less-than-perpendicular angle, creating a diagonal, unclean chop. Viktor struggled to keep hold of the axe. Wood chips flew into the air in all directions.

"Aargh!" exclaimed Viktor as splinters dug into his skin. He felt sharp twinges of pain in his left arm. He glanced down at his arm and saw small wood chips embedded within.

"You have to control the axe. You let the axe control you there. It dragged you with it, and you weren't able to control the angle of impact. That's why that happened," observed Jurgen.

"I'm wounded! Help me! It's inside of me! What if I get infected?" yelled Viktor. Only very rarely had Viktor experienced such pain in his sheltered life in the City. He stood there, staring at the sizable wood chips in his arm, horrified at the thought of something piercing his skin.

The pain was excruciating. Wooden shards embedding themselves into Viktor's previously untainted flesh. Never before had his skin been pierced. This holy sanctum, a product of the City and all its wonders, had finally been infiltrated by the forces of the natural Woods. Tears welled up in Viktor's eyes and though he struggled to keep them from falling, they streamed down both his cheeks.

"It's just a scratch. Here, give me your arm and hold still. No need to cry," replied Jurgen calmly. He came close to Viktor and took out a small knife with a sharp edge.

"Whoa, what are you doing?" asked Viktor, still in agony.

"I'll get the splinters out for you. It's a common accident. Nothing too bad. It'll only take a second," said Jurgen.

"I don't want to do this anymore. Surely there's a better way. Why don't you all use machines? You'd probably be able to get more wood with less effort and less risk and this would never happen to anyone," said Viktor, angry that he had just suffered so much so unnecessarily.

Jurgen smiled. "Not everything is about efficiency. Chopping wood isn't just about producing wood. I genuinely enjoy it. It's always nice to directly feel that you're accomplishing or producing something. You'll share my feeling in no time," replied Jurgen.

"You're saying it's cathartic?" replied Viktor, his tone full of spite.

Jurgen shrugged. "Don't know what that means. It just feels like freedom."

"Well, I certainly don't feel the same way. I'm not going to chop any more wood. *This* is neither fruitful nor cathartic," said Viktor as he motioned to his left arm. He felt simultaneously pained and emasculated. His lips began to pout, and thoughts raced through his head. Thoughts that he wasn't good enough.

Look at me, the so-called "child prodigy" and I can't even do something a gorilla could do. It looks easy but then moving like that must be harder than it looks. If I'm "so smart"— record breaker that I am—I can figure this out. It's just angles and momentum.

His pride hurt. This child prodigy had found something he could not do so easily. He still felt an urge to overcome the hurdle, even though he saw no point or purpose in this specific challenge.

And then another thought.

Jurgen can do it. I'm sure they all can. But I can't. And Alice can't. I'm sure none of us from the City could. And they don't even have HAPOC. Are they just … stronger? Better?

Jurgen's voice broke Viktor's mental musings.

"Are you sure? We can take a break. In any case, let me help you with the splinters. You'll only feel a little pinch. Hold out your arm," said Jurgen.

Viktor looked fearfully at Jurgen's knife but knew that it had to be done, unless he wanted to live with wood chips in his arm for the rest of his life. He had learned of the dangers of a lack of sanitation: infection, gangrene, possible amputation. The government had warned him of the dangers of the Woods. He braced himself and held out his arm.

Jurgen took hold of Viktor's outstretched arm and took out his knife. It was a thing of beauty, sharp as obsidian, glistening in the sunlight. Indeed, Jurgen had sharpened it on his whetstone just yesterday. He moved it slowly toward the splinters in Viktor's arm and finally made contact, digging slowly into the skin to get under the splinter and push it out.

Viktor grimaced and bit his lip, trying not to yell out. The blade cut into Viktor's flesh, and a small streak of red appeared at the point of contact. Viktor tried to keep his arm straight and immobile so that Jurgen could work.

Jurgen moved the knife upward and forced the splinter out.

"There, that wasn't so bad. First one's done, just a few to go," said Jurgen.

But for Viktor, it had been so bad. Only the fear of a gangrenous death gave him the necessary willpower to continue. He knew for certain this was the only way, given the circumstances. Viktor had never experienced pain like this before. HAPOC and the City had seen to that. It had been a protective shield around him, and now that the shield was no more, Viktor felt fragile. Nothing had prepared him for the slightest inconvenience or discomfort. As much as the splinters had hurt, the sensation of the blade burned. He hadn't expected the splinters, so they hadn't instilled in Viktor the psychological panic that the knife had. He watched, anticipating, as the knife slowly entered his body and came out.

Jurgen moved the knife to the next splinter, this one a few inches above the last one. The knife ever so slightly pricked the skin. To Viktor it was torture, a wound that dug deeper into him than it appeared. It wasn't just the physical pain or even the psychological anxiety from anticipating the knife. The worst part was the thoughts in Viktor's mind. That he was inferior to these wild people. He felt like a child, at the mercy of Jurgen's generous hand. Viktor simultaneously appreciated the help yet resented the fact that he was in a position to require help.

The splinter was out, and as Jurgen continued along, taking out splinter after splinter, the thoughts clouded Viktor's head. The physical pain was excruciating for him, and he wondered how Jurgen put up with life in such a state.

As the last splinter came out, Viktor forced out a "Thank you." And then a question to Jurgen. "How'd you know how to fix that? Have you had that happen to you before?"

Jurgen smiled, happy that he could help. "Plenty of times. Almost unavoidable when you're young and trying to learn the art. But I've gotten over that hump now. So will you. It'll get to you sooner or later. I just pick them out myself."

Plenty of times?! Viktor could scarcely bear it once. And he couldn't imagine if he had to be the one using the knife to cut his own skin. He wouldn't be able to do such a thing. Yet Jurgen spoke of himself doing it as if it were nothing.

Viktor continued, his arm still throbbing from the aftermath, "And even though you have to go through that, you still continue chopping?"

"It's really no big deal. Just a few scratches. Besides, the chopping is fun, and it provides wood for the family," Jurgen responded.

No big deal? The thoughts returned to Viktor. What Jurgen did as a simple task felt like a superhuman undertaking for Viktor. The people in the Woods seemed of a different breed. Superior even. At least physically. They staved off pain easily. They looked human, made of the same flesh and blood, but were larger, with arms more than twice as large as Viktor's. Excruciating pain for Viktor was nothing but a scratch for Jurgen. Were they born this way, or was their physical superiority a result of living without HAPOC?

"Let's get back to work," said Jurgen. He picked up the axe by the handle and handed it to Viktor.

"Are you sure I'm ready after all of that?" Viktor was apprehensive. How could Jurgen expect him to go back to doing the deed that had caused him such pain mere seconds after recovery?

"Yeah, trust me, your arm works fine. I could even do it with splinters in my arm," replied Jurgen.

Viktor, driven mostly by pride, forced himself to reach for the axe again. He grabbed it and took it from Jurgen. His palms were sweating, and his mind was filled with fear. But Viktor willed himself to continue to not look weak. The wood was still on the chopping block.

The log was now more than just a log. It represented a challenging enemy to be conquered. A nemesis that had given Viktor a grievous wound that Viktor sought to repay. If he could do this, he would show Jurgen and show himself that he was indeed strong.

So, he wiped the tears from his face and stepped up to the block, reminding himself of Jurgen's example.

"Just slow over your head and focus on the point of contact. Make the axe slide naturally and firmly down into the center of the wood. Hold firm—that way there will be no splinters," Jurgen said.

Viktor, with his arm still throbbing, stepped up and placed his right foot in front of his left, ready to strike. *I can do this. It's simple physics. Hit the wood with the blade at a perpendicular angle.*

Then he brought the axe up behind his back. Blood rushed to his arm as he exerted his muscles to perform this feat. It hurt. The tears came to his eyes again. *You're almost there. Just one more motion. Don't waste this exertion. The pain will amount to something.*

He changed the direction of the force he was exerting on the axe handle with his muscles and now brought the axe down onto the log. He aimed carefully, holding the axe firmly so that it would travel in a straight line and strike at a perpendicular angle. Each additional millisecond holding the axe added to Viktor's agony, but it was all coming to fruition. Now was the moment when it all culminated.

The shining steel of the blade made contact with the center of the wood, cut through it, and embedded itself into the stump that served as a chopping block below. Two equal-sized sections of wood split open on either side of the blade. The wood had been chopped.

Viktor's pain immediately subsided as the adrenaline and endorphins took over. Viktor smiled and whooped a laugh full of pride as well as relief.

"Great job; you did it. See, wasn't so hard, was it?" Jurgen smiled. He went over and threw the split halves to the edge of a small pile of wood.

He had done it. But this one swing had taken so much out of him. He knew that Jurgen could do it, over and over, and could bring the axe over his head and back down hundreds of times without fail, splitting the wood each time, a small victory that only served to reinforce Viktor's grudging respect for Jurgen.

But Viktor felt alive. In a way that he had never felt before. Small beads of sweat were on his skin and small marks of blood on his arm. He looked at the chopped wood, the log that was now split in two because of him. Then he looked at his sweat and blood and made the connection. The chopped wood was a product of those liquids. A product of his work. The wood meant something to him. And he didn't know exactly why. Yet he still looked at it with pride, even though he knew that it was just a block of wood and had very little intrinsic value. Despite the pain, blood, and sweat, Viktor still felt a sense of fulfillment. Or maybe it was because of the pain, blood, and sweat, rather than despite them. The chopped segments were his creation, and his alone. He thought back to Hugo's question. *When was the last time, before you came today to the Woods, that you made a significant decision for yourself, not relying on HAPOC?* The answer was nothing. Nothing was solely his. All that he had done in the past could be credited to HAPOC. Yet this was his labor completely, besides a few words and moments of guidance from Jurgen. And the adversity he faced had made it all the better. It seemed like the sight of the blood and the sweat only served to enhance this warm feeling of fulfillment. He had tackled a great challenge head-on and won in the end. The feeling was a sense of pride that Viktor had never felt before. All over a piece of wood.

And more than that, this was something he had chosen to do. Hugo's question again rang in his ears. *When was the last time, before you came today to the Woods, that you made a significant decision for yourself, not relying on HAPOC?* In the past, everything he did he was told to do because it was the optimal thing for him to do. But this time, he had willed himself to *choose* to do something that not only hurt him but that he also had no desire to do in the beginning. HAPOC had always optimized for his preferences. Now, Viktor had carried out this wood chopping, even though he preferred not to. And he felt good about it. He had encountered adversity for the first time and defeated it, using his own efforts. His will, not HAPOC's, made this happen. He made his own choice, and the fruits of that choice and that labor were sitting in two pieces right in front of him.

The wood chopping had made Viktor's blood rush, unlocking a primordial element of his human nature that had been buried for years under the comforts and conveniences that technology in the City had provided. It was as if a new receptor in his brain had been activated, one that had been dormant but now finally had received its first electrical neural impulses. And now it hungered for more. The brain could no longer be content with just the material pleasures that it had previously enjoyed. It hadn't realized its hunger until it tasted the emotions brought upon by challenge, adversity, and victory.

He felt the same kind of rush he had felt when he and Alice had just entered the Woods. When he had tripped on that root. The pulse through his body that had led him to that heavenly moment.

Why had this never happened before? It seemed so odd. Never before would Viktor have thought that adversity would have any sort of value at all. It was a thing to be avoided, a thing that had been eliminated by HAPOC—a marked triumph of the City. Pain was the enemy, and pleasure was the goal. But this seminal experience with pain, while terrible to begin with, was now beginning to feel potently positive.

These thoughts were all very overwhelming for the child prodigy. So, Viktor decided he would sort them out later, make sense of these new sensations at a different time. For now, Viktor wanted to know one thing that had been on his mind for a while.

"Thanks, but now you have to tell me about your father," Viktor said.

"I did say I'd do that if you chopped the wood, didn't I?" replied Jurgen.

"Indeed, you did."

"Well, what do you want to know?"

"How'd he come to be here? What did he do before, when he was in the City?"

"I'll tell you, but it's a long story, so listen up."

They made their way to two stumps and sat down. Then Jurgen spoke, and Viktor listened.

CHAPTER IX

———

Viktor had a million thoughts racing in his mind about Hugo. He was the mysterious man who had welcomed them, given them shelter, and showed them kindness. He was also the man who showed an aversion to HAPOC, someone who had left the wonders of the City to live in this backwoods. Was he a crazy man? A traitor? An enemy of the state? Yet he was good to Viktor and Alice, and Viktor saw that he was built of the same strong fiber that Jurgen was made of.

"My father Hugo is a simple man," said Jurgen. "He was born in the City. He grew up there as you did and lived with the same technological tools that you live with. Now he lives here in the Woods with our community and is simply a man who works to provide for his family, much like the rest of us."

"How did he come to be here if he lived in the City?" asked Viktor.

"By chance, when he was a young man, he was part of a rare government-led excursion into the Woods. He got lost after he separated from the group. They searched for him but left him for dead when they couldn't find him. But he ended up here, with the people of the Woods," said Jurgen.

"And how did the people of the Woods come to be?"

"Some of us lived here before the construction of the Wall around the City and now live here apart from the Wall. Some of us, like my father, came from the City. But we're just our simple community. We don't bother the City and they don't bother us. Every now and then, they send us some people who would rather live with us. It's a great place to live."

Viktor struggled to hide a smirk. The implication, ever so slight, that Jurgen enjoyed living in the Woods more than the City sounded ridiculous to Viktor. He had a chance to regain the pride he had lost while chopping wood. He would convince Jurgen of his inferiority.

"Your simple community … it's a rather ascetic lifestyle, isn't it?" asked Viktor.

"I don't know what that word means," said Jurgen.

"You lack the comforts and niceties of life in the City. It's not as prosperous here by a long stretch," said Viktor.

Jurgen made a face at Viktor's condescending statement. "Well, I was born here in the Woods, so I only know what my father has told me about the City. It sounds like a lavish hell from what I've heard," he replied.

"Hell? This place is much more brutish. Your life would be so much better if you lived in the City. There'd be no need to chop wood, for one," Viktor asserted.

"Then what's the worst thing you've experienced in the City?"

Viktor thought for a moment. His only memories were happy, for he had never done something that he hadn't wanted to do.

"Nothing comes to mind."

"So that wood chopping—it must have been a pretty hefty task for you," said Jurgen.

Viktor still felt the pain in his arm. Memories of the splinters entering his arm and Jurgen's knife cutting into his flesh resurfaced in his mind.

"That's probably the worst thing I've experienced. Nothing like that would ever happen to you in the City," replied Viktor. "And what do you need to do in the City?" asked Jurgen. "Nothing really. You can just do what you want. HAPOC will take care of the rest. Life's great that way. We're all happy there. No pain, no suffering. Only positive things." Viktor smiled with pride as he thought of the fair share of work he was doing to help create such a utopia.

"And what do you want to do?"

"I like computers. I work on the HAPOC system actually."

"And how'd you come to do that?" asked Jurgen.

"I was born for it. I was born smart, and I was born to be great at working with computers. HAPOC knew that. It's clearly the optimal job for me, and I love it."

"So, you were assigned to the job?"

"Yeah, but only because I wanted it. I knew I'd be good for it. All the tests and calculations determined that. It's what makes me intellectually stimulated, and it's what I would be good at."

Viktor thought back to when he was younger. At age six, he had been identified by HAPOC as having a bright mind, great for technical analyses and algorithmic work. The brightest in his peer group, in fact. From then on, he had been given exercises and activities to groom him for the job he would eventually have, all of which he had found fascinating. As he entered his teenage years, the initial hypothesis was only confirmed by the years of data HAPOC had collected. This was the job for him. He loved it and prided himself on it.

Jurgen interrupted his pleasant reflection. "But how'd you know that would be the job for you?"

"It has to be. That's what all the data says. And that stuff is always right. Any other job would be suboptimal." Viktor replied.

"So, you were told that this was it, and you accepted it."

"Yes, and it proved to be totally right! As it always is. No surprise there. That's how everyone in the City gets jobs. That's why we're so productive. Everyone is doing the thing they'd be best at and that they'd be happy with. Our talents are put to the best use. HAPOC knows what's best." Viktor tried hard to highlight the wonders of the City for Jurgen.

"Have you ever tried anything else?"

"No. Why would I? That would be pointless. Everything else wouldn't be as good. I'm certain of that. HAPOC is certain of it too."

"My father had asked you a question before we came out here to chop wood, and you didn't seem able to come up with an answer, so I'm curious and I'll ask you again—when was the last time you made a significant decision for yourself, not relying on HAPOC?"

Viktor had had ample time to think about Hugo's question. He had an aggressive answer, one that would show the true superiority of the City.

"Never! That's the beauty of it. I don't have to do that. HAPOC does it for me. But you do. You and your father and everyone here has to be burdened by the weight of choice. You never know what's the right decision. You're uninformed. All the decisions we make in the City are perfectly informed. We make the best decisions. You can't say the same." Viktor smiled haughtily.

Jurgen looked offended, yet unsurprised. He probed deeper. "So, you view your lack of choice as an advantage?" "Definitely. Choice only exists out of uncertainty. Once you have certainty, there's only one choice. The certain one." Yet even as Viktor emphatically voiced these declarations of faith in HAPOC, seeds of doubt were growing in his mind. The wood chopping had given him an injection of new sensations. Pleasant ones. But not pleasure like the hedonistic way of life in the City. Somehow, the bleeding and sweating and the pain had given him a small sense of awakening. Together with the finished and cut blocks of wood, they created an experience that made Viktor feel more whole than anything he had done before. And the knowledge that it was his choice—that he was personally responsible for what had transpired—made the experience feel true.

"Yet you made the choice to chop the wood, even though you clearly didn't want to, and the outcome seems 'suboptimal' compared to what you described with machines doing all the labor while you do whatever you want," Jurgen stated.

"Yeah, I did. It definitely would have been better if we had a machine. This is suboptimal. Just look what happened to my arm!"

"Maybe. But tell me how it makes you feel," probed Jurgen.

Viktor paused. If he told Jurgen how it really made him feel, he would be undermining his own argument. Maybe Jurgen had a point. Some unquantifiable element was missing that HAPOC couldn't provide. The competing ideas in his head made Viktor uncomfortable, and he searched for consistency among his thoughts. A new seed was growing, and it was tearing up the roots that had been there before.

So, Viktor responded, "Well ... I feel ... good. I think I felt what you meant when you said you enjoyed it. It was cathartic. I liked the fact that I willed myself to do something hard that I didn't like and that I achieved something out of it. But it's more than just catharsis I feel. There's fulfillment," admitted Viktor.

"But if it caused you so much pain and trouble, was it worth it?"

"My mind wants to say a definite 'no,' but my body actually likes it. I think it's because of the feeling of accomplishment when I witness the attestation of my labor."

Jurgen began, "Yes. Things turn out sweeter when you work for them. When I feel my muscles throb and I see my pile of wood, it feels good. The fact that I've done something of value. It feels even better than just having someone give the wood to me for free. It feels earned. It was my choice and my work. It feels like I've conquered something."

Viktor replied, touching half of the log he chopped. "It's as if this wood were somehow more than just wood, and it's imbued with the effort that I put in to earn it." He gazed at the chopped wood. His arm felt better now. The sensation of pain felt better, like how the soreness in Jurgen's muscles could make him feel a certain type of high.

Some commotion was heard at the door to the cabin. Viktor looked up from his chopped log to see Hugo emerging from the entryway to the yard. He smiled a wide, avuncular smile and walked toward Viktor and Jurgen.

"Ah, so it looks like you've enjoyed the work. I couldn't help but overhear your conversation. Tell me, do you get this kind of experience in the City?" Hugo asked.

Viktor thought for a moment. This experience in the Woods had been nothing like anything he had experienced in the City. Somehow, he had found the adversity ... enriching.

He replied slowly, "No ..."

"Why not?"

"There's never an opportunity to make the choice to work. Everything is done for you. And everything is so nice— there's no discomfort of any sort to be confronted." Jurgen remarked. "Sounds like a boring place. Nothing to overcome. Nowhere to fight the good fight."

"The good fight?" Viktor was unfamiliar with the term. Jurgen took a stern look at Viktor with piercing eyes. "The good fight. Taking on the challenges that the world throws at you and taking them in stride. Achieving things out of a good struggle. Coming out stronger."

"You're saying that discomfort enhances life?"

"Yeah, it makes those of us who can deal with it stronger. Look how weak you are and look how strong I am," Jurgen said in a matter-of-fact tone.

"You really think those splinters were no big deal? And you get them all the time?"

"Exactly my point. A babe in the Woods wouldn't have cried as much as you did," said Jurgen.

Hugo added, "In the City, you're made weak by your comfort. You're denied any opportunity to truly grow. Some hardship is required for health. Some sickness is required to strengthen your immune system. Without rain there can be no rainbows. We are creatures that grow from discomfort. It helps us learn. In your City's quest to eliminate all that's negative and pursue only what's 'perfect' and 'optimal,' it has given up that which is essential to human nature. That's what I learned here and why I decided to leave the City for good. Do you understand now, Viktor?" Hugo gazed into Viktor's eyes, as if he were trying to take the measure of Viktor's spirit and imprint in it his own ideals.

Viktor felt Hugo's words seep deep into his soul. And though he could see that Hugo was right about the value of adversity, he still had some doubts. The adrenaline and shock from the wood chopping was wearing off, and Viktor began to remember and think about his home in the City.

"I understand, Hugo. I learned a lot today. But what about all the advances made in the City that have afforded thousands with happier, more comfortable lives? Surely HAPOC has some value, even a tremendous amount, one could argue?" Viktor replied.

"Yes, undoubtedly life is harsher here. But it's what I prefer. The material comforts of your City mean nothing to me if my basic human needs haven't been catered to. Life isn't meant to be lived by cowards. I require struggle—the good fight—in my life. HAPOC has created a beautiful decorated life on the exterior, but, on the inside, it's empty."

Viktor nodded slowly as he let Hugo's words marinate in his mind.

Hugo turned to his son. "Jurgen, thank you for your help. Now please follow me. Bring the wood, we'll need it."

CHAPTER X

Hearing Hugo's words, Jurgen went to the pile of wood, a dutiful son acting out of love for his father and family. He playfully looked at Viktor, knowing that the youth was weak from life in the City, challenging him with his eyes to see if he could lift the log. The strongman then went to work and displayed his strength. He squatted down, took a few logs between his arms, and lifted them up.

He turned to Viktor and smiled, seemingly unstrained by the physical task at hand. "Why don't you grab the log you just chopped?"

Viktor was dreading this. After such exertion, there was still more to do? His face formed into a visible grimace, but he followed the order anyway, dragging his feet toward the pile.

Seeing the displeasure on Viktor's face, Jurgen, still holding his load, said some words of encouragement. "Don't worry, if you were strong enough to swing the axe, you're more than strong enough to carry a log. Go reap the fruits of your labor."

Viktor came to a stop right in front of the two halves of the log that he had split. Jurgen had thrown them toward the pile as if they were made of nothing, and Viktor hoped that they would be indeed as lightweight as his new friend had made them seem.

He bent down and embraced the log halves with his arms. He felt the rough and jagged bark, the source of the splinters, the source of his pain. But he had triumphed over it, cutting it down with an axe. And from that act, he gained fulfillment. To touch the wood was to bring himself closer to the feeling.

Viktor tried to lift with his arms, his scrawny muscles flexing and pale blue lines appearing against the backdrop of his milky white forearms in the process.

The logs lifted a few inches off of the ground, but the load quickly became too heavy and Viktor set it down again.

He had to put his whole body into it. Repositioning himself, he squatted and bent over, this time using his legs and back to lift the logs off the ground. Sensations of personal pride rushed through his body. The successful act had made him feel less inadequate and calmed his internal insecurities.

"Great work! Now follow me," said Jurgen. He and Hugo walked through the yard parallel to a side of the cabin, and then turned at the corner of the structure to enter into a new side of the yard.

Viktor struggled to mimic Jurgen's graceful, effortless walk. But his body ached. Though he held two logs to Jurgen's six, Viktor struggled. He could feel the lactic acid building up in his muscles. He willed himself forward. Viktor wanted nothing more than to drop the logs where he stood, but he pushed himself to keep walking. This was a conflicting feeling he'd never experienced before in the City where all was decided for him.

They found themselves in an area that served as the kitchen. In front of the men was an open pot of iron hanging over a small pile of unlit logs. These logs were encircled by stones, creating a fire pit. Jurgen deposited his load onto this pile, and Viktor hurriedly spilled his into the pile as well. Relief spread through Viktor's body, intensifying in his arms.

"Thank you to the two of you for that. Jurgen, you can go back to chopping some more wood in the yard. Viktor and I can take it from here," said Hugo. The son walked into the yard to pick up the axe again.

Hugo then turned to Viktor and smiled that avuncular smile. "Thank you for the wood, Viktor. We'll need it to cook supper."

Cook? This was a foreign concept to Viktor. Food production in the City was fully automated. HAPOC could prepare any mixture of foods and ingredients with better precision and personalization than any human chef could. That way, food could be optimized perfectly to one's tastes and dietary needs.

But these strange people from the Woods seemed to prepare their own food. *How unsanitary,* thought Viktor.

"How will the wood help us cook supper?" asked Viktor, unaware of the crude ways of the Woods.

Hugo stepped in to calmly explain the concept to the foreigner. "We burn the wood, and it gives us a source of intense heat with which we can cook our foods, thus killing bacteria, developing flavor, and making it ready for human consumption."

Viktor understood. It was the same fundamental scientific concept he had learned in different contexts. Use combustion to generate heat, and then use that heat for biological purposes. The City simply did this with a much more efficient energy source than wood. Even the fossil fuels used by primitive societies of mankind's past far outstripped the energy potential of wood. But in theory, this would work.

He would place his trust in science and participate in this primitive cooking.

"I understand the science; thank you for explaining. So, will we start burning the logs now?" replied Viktor, trying to cover up the ignorance he had let slip.

Hugo smiled as he noticed the desperate, instinctive maneuver employed to save face. "No, we need to prepare the food first. We'll get everything ready and put it in the pot; then, we'll start the fire underneath."

"Yes, of course, to be more efficient with the energy source," Viktor paused, thinking it through in his head. "What food are we preparing?" he continued.

"We have some venison and some poultry we brought back from a hunt in the forest. Which one would you prefer?" asked Hugo.

Viktor paused. He didn't know what venison was, so how could he make a decision? All the choices he had made in the City had been perfectly informed, but this was a shot in the dark. What if he chose wrong?

"What's venison? I'd like to learn more about the meats before I choose."

On Hugo's face was a knowing grin. He seemed to see right through Viktor. "Yes, it's always good to know more before we commit to a choice. Venison is, quite simply, deer meat. You've heard of deer, right?"

Viktor remembered his first encounter with a deer, just a few hours ago. His brows furrowed as he contemplated the fact that those beasts were eaten by humans. "I saw one for the first time today. I didn't know that people ate them."

"It's quite tasty. Tender, moist, and flavorful. A real treat. Is there more you'd like to know before you make your choice?" asked Hugo.

"Tons more. When we make decisions in the City, we're fully informed. Typically, I would know the nutritional content of each food item, the compatibility with my digestive and other bodily systems, the degree to which it would stimulate my taste buds, and much more. But you don't know all of that, do you?" Viktor sighed. He spoke in a tone of superiority, and his words sought to convey the inferiority of the Woods.

"Indeed, we don't. We make our own choices here, we don't count on an algorithm to tell us how to act or what to eat," Hugo added in a subtle jab of his own. "You're right that we don't have all that information, but we live life freely, which is something you cannot claim. So, tell me, what will it be?"

Viktor froze. Hugo had him in a corner. He couldn't choose, not without information or a guide like HAPOC. The fear of choosing wrong loomed over him.

"I'm leaning toward poultry, but there's no basis for that. It's just a gut instinct, and my mind and body are imperfect. I guess I know that eggs come from chicken, and I do like eggs and know that they're healthy. But how can I choose when there's such a high risk of being wrong?" Viktor blurted out.

"Just make a choice and stand by it. Mistakes are a part of life. We live and we learn. But the important thing to do now is to choose," said Hugo with an air of wisdom.

"But mistakes aren't part of life in the City!" Viktor protested. His voice grew louder.

"That's because you can't make a mistake if you aren't the one deciding. You let HAPOC decide and you escape from the fear of being wrong, choosing to trade freedom for certainty," said Hugo resolutely.

"I know to listen to superior information—HAPOC is always right, why should I deviate from it?" challenged Viktor. Hugo, though old, didn't miss a beat. "Because to act, to choose, and to be free are inalienable things. Nothing is worth giving them up. Not even certainty. Only those who are weak would take such an easy escape," he replied.

The insult was felt. After his experience chopping wood, Viktor did indeed feel weak. In a way, these men and women in the Woods were considerably stronger than he and his compatriots in the City. They could so easily carry out tasks that would be incredibly difficult for City dwellers. Was what Hugo saying indeed the reason why? Viktor took a moment to think, and a crisp silence filled the air.

Hugo seized the initiative, "One cannot grow without mistakes, nor without the freedom to make them. To have your own skin in the game of life is what makes life worth living. You lack many things, but, above all, you lack will, and you're full of fear. A life subordinated to HAPOC has left you stunted."

The harsh words rang in Viktor's ears. The defense mechanisms kicked in. He could feel the anger swelling, the chemicals rushing to his brain. But his scientifically attuned mind knew there was truth in those words. The experiences of the day served as data points attesting to that truth.

But before he could reply, Hugo added, in a conciliatory tone, "I want to help you. I want to give you the power we have. To help you to be able to swing axes, cook food, and choose."

Viktor's thoughts turned to the axe. It was a powerful tool not just because of its capacity to cut and do damage but also because of what it embodied for Viktor. It was a tool that required will and hard work to wield, yet it repaid those efforts with fulfillment and strength. He thought about the rush that it had given him, something he had never felt before in the City. Hugo didn't lie. Indeed, emotions would be felt, experiences would be had, and strength would be gained through Hugo's way of life.

Viktor made up his mind. He thought about his words before he said them. "I see; you're saying I need to choose because, by choosing, I exercise my free will and I embrace risk. And dealing with the ensuing uncertainty will make me stronger; even more than that, just choosing to face the fear of uncertainty head on is valuable in and of itself."

Hugo nodded approvingly. "Yes, exactly. Your life will be less comfortable as a result. Things will go wrong. You'll make mistakes, but so long as we trudge on gracefully in the face of whatever life throws our way, our lives will be purposeful—"

"I want to be strong like that. I want to be strong like you. Let me start now. I choose … the venison," Viktor leapt in.

CHAPTER XI

———

Viktor had chosen the venison. The meat of the Woods. The unknown. Whether it would taste good or bad, he decided he would own the consequences. The important part was making the choice. This was the plunge.

He remembered Hugo's question from earlier in the day: *When was the last time that you made a significant decision for yourself, not relying on HAPOC?* Well, this would certainly count as an answer to the question. Because of him, the entire meal of a family was decided. He made the call. Inside, Viktor still feared that his choice was suboptimal, that the needs and tastes of Hugo's family would not be sufficiently met.

Hugo chimed in, "Great choice, Viktor. Great that you even made a choice, for that matter. Let's get cooking then! Stay here." He walked out of the room with a spring to his step, and quickly came back holding a slab of meat that was shaped approximately like a square, red in color, with white streaks of fat running through it. He placed it on top of a counter. Viktor walked over to take a closer look.

"Here's the meat! Help me prepare it."

Viktor replied, "What can I do?"

"Help me make some culinary choices. First question: should we cut it into small pieces or cook it whole?"

Viktor gazed at the piece of meat and thought for a moment. He gave an instinctive answer guided by his limited knowledge of thermodynamics, but one that lacked the certainty of a decree by HAPOC. "Let's cut it into small pieces. That way, the heat transfer will be faster, and it will cook quicker."

The weathered woodsman nodded. Acting on Viktor's recommendation, Hugo opened a wooden drawer and pulled out a knife. "Good idea, why don't you do it?" Hugo handed the knife to Viktor.

Viktor took it and acted on his decision. A jolt of energy shot through his body. He held the knife, just as he held the axe. He had reached out and taken it. The act of will sent a surge of power through his knife arm.

He went to work. Holding the meat down with his left hand, Viktor began to cut straight lines into it with the knife in his right. Operating the knife with his right hand gave him the same feeling as wielding the axe did. With his left, he could feel the stickiness of the raw meat—unpleasant, but he carried on.

Six vertical and six horizontal cuts later, thirty-six small chunks were made. Viktor's left hand was also covered in deer blood.

"Thank you so much, Viktor. Let me get you some water." Hugo stepped out again, this time coming back with a bucket of water and a bar of soap. "Wash your hands with this water and soap."

Viktor dipped his hands into the water, proceeding to rub them together with the soap to get the blood off. He withdrew his hands. They were clean, and the water was now a reddish color.

"Next choice: salt or sugar?" asked Hugo.

Viktor replied, letting his own mind choose. "Let's use sugar. I always liked sweet things." He was having fun now, picking and choosing. He felt powerful, like he was now HAPOC, the director of his own world. He felt pleasure from exercising his own will. It wasn't a hedonistic pleasure like those of the City but one that gave him inner strength.

Hugo acquiesced, grabbing a pouch from another room and sprinkling sugar from that pouch onto the freshly cut chunks of meat.

"Third: Cook it in the pot or on skewers over the open fire?"

Viktor chose the pot. Hugo poured the meat into it.

"Thank you for your help, Viktor; I'll take it from here," said Hugo. He walked over to the pile of logs encircled by stones that served as a fire pit. Hugo spread some kindling in the form of dry leaves in the center. Then, he organized a few logs into a tent shape, having them support each other as they stood up. He pulled out flint and steel from his pocket. Striking the flint with the steel, Hugo made sparks fly and land onto the kindling. They caught fire, igniting in a dance of red and orange, and the conflagration quickly spread to the sturdier logs, creating a sustained blaze.

Flames leapt up to lick the bottom of the pot. Viktor could feel the heat emanating, and knew that soon enough, the meat would be cooked.

"Give it some time; it'll be ready soon, given how small the chunks were and how large this fire is in comparison," remarked Hugo. "Are you excited to eat?"

Viktor gazed into the flames. They were there, in part, because of the log he chopped, and the meat lay in the pot the way it was because of his choices. "I'm excited ..." He paused and looked up at Hugo, like a child looking for reassurance. "What if it tastes bad, though? What if it doesn't fulfill your nutritional needs? What if the poultry would have been better?"

The satisfied teacher chuckled, "I guarantee you it'll be edible, at the very least. And besides, regardless of how it tastes or what's inside, it's your creation—a product of your work and your choices. Trust yourself. If it turns out poorly, it won't be the end of the world."

These were new ideas to Viktor. He had been afraid to choose his whole life because making a mistake in the City was very much the end of the world. The specter of suboptimality loomed over every decision, so HAPOC was created to usher it away.

Hugo's trained hands continued to tend to the pot, making sure the meat was cooked appropriately. Soon enough, it was ready. Hugo took the chunks out of the pot and onto a plate.

He took one and blew on it hard so that it would cool. "Try some," Hugo said.

Viktor grabbed a piece with his hand. It was hot to the point of discomfort, though not pain. Viktor blew on it to cool it, plopped it into his mouth, and chewed.

As his molars bit down into the meat, the gamey, wild taste of the venison exploded into Viktor's mouth. It was unlike anything he had ever tasted. Rich, almost overwhelming flavors tickled his taste buds. His choice of sugar added a sweet twist, creating a unique blend of gustatory sensations. It was a taste Viktor could stomach, though not one that he particularly enjoyed. Yet aside from the hedonistic aspect of the food, he felt something now that he had never felt in all the perfectly optimized foods of the City. The flavors weren't merely flavors. What the tongue had lost, the spirit had gained. This was nourishment for the soul. This was Viktor's creation, born of the choices that he had made. For the first time, he was no longer just a cog in a machine, but the director of his own body. He took responsibility for the suboptimal taste and embraced it. The fear of failure was overcome, and Viktor took in the full sensations of the food: flavor, fulfillment, and freedom.

"How is it?" asked Hugo.

Viktor responded, "It could taste better; that's for sure ... Yet, I still find myself enjoying this bite more than any bite I've ever had."

Hugo smiled brightly at Viktor, "That's the taste of freedom. You're responsible for this creation. And because of that fact, you're feeling fulfilled. Only through facing our fears head on, taking responsibility, and working hard can we live a full life."

Viktor let the words marinate. "Maybe you're right."

"I'm proud of you, Viktor." Hugo got up, standing straight like a champion who had just conquered an opponent. "Why don't we go back in for now? Let's see what my wife and your friend have been up too. Then, we can share what you've created with everyone!"

So, they made their way back into the house of logs.

CHAPTER XII

———

Inside once again, walls made of brown wood surrounded Viktor and Hugo on all sides. But now Viktor looked upon the rustic cabin with a newfound sense of appreciation. Chopping one log had been so difficult, yet this structure was made of hundreds of logs. No doubt, it was hand-built, a product of the labors of humans, not machine.

Already seated at the circular table were Alice and Hugo's wife, Sophia, back from their time sewing together. On the table was a sewing kit. A needle was stuck into a spool of yarn, and a small, half-finished quilt covered the corner of the table. Viktor looked at Alice's hand and saw a noticeable red mark. Like him, she had suffered, the needle penetrating her skin. She looked unhappy. Her eyes ceased to gleam.

Hugo, Jurgen, and Viktor took their seats at the table.

"We appreciate your help with our household chores," Hugo began, speaking to Viktor and Alice.

"We appreciate the shelter and hospitality," Viktor returned the compliment.

"Did you two have a good time today?" asked Hugo.

Viktor flashed his teeth and Alice's chin flexed in a frown. Simultaneously they replied:

"Yes!" exclaimed Viktor.

"No," said Alice.

Viktor and Alice looked at each other, confused. They were experiencing friction in their relationship. This wasn't supposed to happen.

"What happened?" Viktor asked.

"I want to go home, Viktor. It's been terrible. A needle punctured my skin and it hurt so much. Everything's so hard here, so crude."

Viktor tried to convince her of his truth. "But you made that quilt, right? Aren't you proud of that?"

"So what? It's useless. Why would that be worth anything? It certainly isn't worth what I went through to create it."

"Oh," said Viktor.

Hugo, Jurgen, and Sophia sat silently, tacitly watching the lovers' quarrel.

"I miss the City where life is good. Can we go back soon?" asked Alice.

"I actually like it here. Everything is just more … real. It makes me feel more alive, more fulfilled. Awakens my spirit of achievement."

"What does that even mean, Viktor? Everything is more *real*? How can you prefer these abstract concepts to the tangible comforts and goods that we're able to enjoy in the City?" Alice replied, incredulous.

"The City is nice and all, but it doesn't satisfy my fundamental needs. Needs that I didn't discover that I even had until today. I need to feel like I have free will, that I have choice over what I do. And I need to feel that I earn the things I receive," Viktor said.

Alice glared at him. Viktor's words had come across to her as childish and immature, and she grew angry at the thought that the man whom she had been so in sync with just hours ago was now so different. The words he had uttered were so antithetical to what she believed. So, she became cold to Viktor. Arms crossed, she spoke to him in a harsh and condescending tone.

"You're weird, Viktor. Such ridiculous notions. You're ungrateful; you know that? This trip made me so much more grateful for what we have in the City. For what HAPOC provides us. In the City, we have lives that are degrees of magnitude more prosperous and comfortable than what we experienced today. Yet, you would throw all that away to satisfy some silly notions in your head."

Viktor sighed. He saw how visibly upset Alice was. He certainly felt the temptations of the comforts of the City, but his will to power over his own life was stronger. And he realized that Alice wasn't for him. She was a City girl, but his heart belonged in the Woods. HAPOC had been offline and hadn't been able to recalibrate and direct them during their time in the Woods, so the matching system had fallen out of whack. The AMOUR pills had also worn off.

He was heartbroken. They could never work. But the feelings from earlier that day still lingered. His face turned red, his eyebrows wilted, and his shoulders slumped. A bleak figure in front of Alice.

She noticed it too, and she calmed down. Uncrossing her arms, she placed a hand on his shoulder. Viktor was still the man whom she had shared her first kiss with, but she knew he had changed, and it wouldn't be the same as before.

"Let's just go home and forget about all of this, okay? Let's go back to that Egg Café," Alice said in a more conciliatory tone. She felt a conflict inside of her regarding Viktor.

Viktor had no desire to return to the Egg Café or to any part of the City, but he knew that he must. He had obligations. Parents, a job, friends, and more—all awaited his return. And he felt a responsibility to take Alice back, since he was the one who convinced her to come out here in the first place.

In the midst of this emotional exchange, Viktor regained awareness of his surroundings. Hugo and Jurgen were still there, just watching.

Viktor turned to Hugo and Jurgen. "I owe you a ton. Thank you so much for all you've done for us. I would love to stay, but we need to return. Please enjoy the supper."

Hugo replied, "I'm glad you found your time here illuminating. Maybe you'll be back here before you know it." Hugo smiled and the wrinkles on his face grew deeper. He had managed to help one of the two visitors see another side of life. He liked the young man and would be sad to see him leave.

At this, Viktor and Alice got up out of their chairs and walked slowly out of the house. Viktor looked back and smiled a bittersweet smile, while Alice marched on out. Hugo waved back, making eye contact with Viktor. They shared a final glance and Viktor hurried to catch up with Alice, who hadn't spent the time on these niceties and so was already a few paces ahead.

They walked back through the forest to the gate in silence. Their philosophical differences were obvious to each other, and not much more could be said.

Though there was one thing that remained on Viktor's mind. Their kiss, their shared moment of tenderness and vulnerability—surely that meant something to Alice. It certainly meant something to him, and that meaning was slowly making itself known through the moisture that began to appear in his eyes.

They walked back along the path from whence they came. Back into the forest, whose verdant greens now seemed drab as the sun sat lower in the sky and the light was weaker. On they trudged through the foliage and dirt, this time walking side by side but no longer holding hands. Each step for Viktor felt heavy, for he had an inkling that these steps would be the last that they shared. But she was walking so fast, as if she were trying to end the ordeal as soon as possible and get away from him. She seemed revolted by the ideas he had expressed back in Hugo's home

And then they arrived at a familiar scene. A familiar tree with distinctive branches gave the location away. It was the very spot where they had their moment.

Viktor stopped in his tracks. A flood of emotions came over him. Sadness and heartache. Two more emotions to add to the others that he had experienced today for the first time. He felt a pain emanating from his core, yet he hadn't been wounded or injured. But the sharp sting was there nonetheless. It started at his heart and poured into the rest of his body,

Alice had noticed that Viktor had stopped walking and she stood in place as well, waiting for him. She looked at him impatiently.

Viktor looked up slowly and spoke in a trembling voice, "What about our kiss? You said yourself that something that great would have never happened in the City."

She looked back at him and sighed. Her eyes looked down to the ground, and when they came back up to look at him, they looked softer and gentler, like they did when they were last in this setting.

"That was a nice feeling, Viktor. But look at how we feel now. It's terrible. No one should ever have to feel this way. And no one does in the City," said Alice as she hurt inside.

"That's what makes it real, Alice!" exclaimed Viktor in desperation.

She looked at him with confusion. "I just don't understand you, Viktor. Life is real enough in the City. There's no need for this. We can just go back and make it all better."

Viktor thought about the prospect. A life with Alice in the City, with nothing to worry about. He'd be happy and shielded from all the misfortunes of life. It sounded pleasant. But it would be so boring. Viktor's body itched for challenge now. To conquer and to achieve. He would find no chance of that in the City. It wouldn't feel right otherwise.

"That's not real, Alice. We'd wake up every day when HAPOC tells us to, eat what HAPOC feeds us, and do whatever HAPOC says. Sure, maybe it'd lead to the optimal outcome, but I don't want that. If you remove all that's exciting and valuable in life—if you remove all the risk and uncertainty—then everything becomes dull. I want to create my own life, to chop my own wood and cook my own food," replied Viktor.

The gentleness disappeared from Alice's face and was now replaced with incredulity.

She put her foot down. Viktor was beyond saving. "Chop your own wood? Cook your own food? You sound like a madman. Never mind; it's hopeless. Let's walk back. There's nothing to talk about between us."

The final nail had been hammered into the coffin. Viktor was now totally alone. The one he had felt so intensely for was now completely disconnected from him, and the reason was precisely that she wouldn't allow herself to feel as intensely as him. To do so would expose her to the downside, to the risk of being hurt. She had been hurt and felt the heartbreak and decided that never again would she allow that to happen. Better for Alice to live the pleasant, protected life within the City. Viktor knew that this was how things were now. No one from the City would understand him. No one would understand what he went through. They were all obsessed with optimality. The citizenry of hedonists who sought to avoid pain at every instance would surely never understand its value. They would, like Alice, view his desire to take risk, to overcome challenges, and to earn things as the stupid, suboptimal fantasies of a deranged madman.

Viktor felt alone, and he was about to reenter a world where he would be even more alone.

So, they continued in silence, walking back through the gate again and calling vehicles to take them back to their respective homes. Clearly, they would never see each other again.

Viktor returned to his bed and fell asleep, exhausted from the day.

CHAPTER XIII

———

Back in the comfort of his own home in the City, Viktor fell into a deep sleep. Fatigued by the epiphanic events of the day, his mind wandered its way into strange settings.

He awoke in that grassy field again. With his fingers he could feel the sharp yet soft blades of grass. He felt his back resting on a bed of leaves. In the distance, he could hear birdsong. The sound was as gentle as feathers.

Viktor sat up, and his field of vision shifted from whites and blues of the sky to the greens and browns of the field. In front of him was a dirt path, a brown line that cut through the green plane of grass. Following the path with his eyes, he saw that it led toward the Woods into the distance. Looking the other way, the path led back to the Gate that surrounded the City.

It was just like in life. He and Alice had walked down that path, away from the Gate and toward the Woods, and in the few hours following that fateful decision, serious doubts about his life in the City were planted and had grown in Viktor's mind.

Viktor stood straight up, stepping off the grassy knoll and onto the dirt path. It was the only artificial thing there, a scar through the natural peace of the place. Yet, in one direction also lay the City. From this distance, the Gate looked almost completely straight with no curvature, even though Viktor knew it to be a structure that encircled the City. It guarded a massive behemoth, keeping the burdens of nature from affecting the prosperous lives of the people within. But it also enclosed those people within, preventing them from expanding into and ravaging the Woods. Or maybe it was meant to keep the people inside, under the watchful eyes of the Council of Overseers. It was the gateway to his entire life up to the fateful trip into the Woods, a life that he once felt was perfect.

He turned and looked the other way. Now, in front of him in the distance were the Woods. A place of danger and primitive living, but also so beautiful.

His feet began to move, and he walked forward onto the path. He was perpendicular to it, and all that was left for him to do was to choose a direction to turn. Back to the comfort of the City, or into the antediluvian Woods?

Deciding to play it safe, he commanded his legs to turn back home, toward the City where he was born and raised. However tantalizing the Woods may be, he knew that he was guaranteed a good life in the City. He thought about how grateful he should be to have been born in the City, to be among the most prosperous people who had ever walked the earth.

But his feet didn't budge. They didn't respond to his neural commands. Instead, they turned the opposite way, and now Viktor was facing the Woods. His feet began to walk forward, and Viktor couldn't stop them. As if controlled by a higher power, Viktor could only accept the path that had been chosen for him.

Soon, he passed the tree line. The same vibrant colors filled his field of vision. Walking further, he happened upon the village, and he soon entered into Hugo's backyard. No one was there but, in the center, he saw a tree stump with an axe sticking in it.

A familiar face came into view—a tall figure with burly features: Hugo. He spoke, "Take the axe."

Viktor obeyed. This time, his body listened to his mind's commands. He stepped forward, took hold of the axe with two hands, and pulled it out of the stump. With the wooden handle now in his hand, Viktor felt a surge of energy. He felt powerful now. He was in control of his actions.

Spotting a nearby log, Viktor took it and placed it onto the stump. Then, in one motion, he brought the axe down upon it, splitting it in two. Adrenaline rushed through his veins.

Hugo spoke again, "The power is yours now. Few of you from the City ever possess this. Use it wisely."

Viktor awoke.

CHAPTER XIV

Still shaken from yesterday and fresh out of his reverie, Viktor awoke at the wrong time, 7:00:00 instead of 6:20:24. The previous day without HAPOC had thrown off the algorithm. HAPOC hadn't been able to adjust for the fatiguing experiences Viktor had. As a result, he had slept through the previously set alarm at 6:20:24. Worse still, Viktor would be late for work.

Realizing this, Viktor bolted out of bed and rushed through his morning routine, ignoring HAPOC's recommendations and striving only for speed. He wore the first thing he could find, skipped breakfast, and brushed his teeth for only one minute. It wasn't optimal to say the least.

Viktor exited the house and hopped in an auto. As it took him through the City, Viktor began to calm down as he sat in the auto and looked outside. HAPOC noticed too, reporting that his heart rate had returned to normal.

The outside City, once beautiful and magnificent to Viktor, now looked rigid and uncompromising. Men and women walked the streets, robotically heading to their respective destinations. They moved perfectly as clockwork, and as soullessly.

As Viktor stepped out of his auto in front of the domineering Corinthian columns that marked the entrance to the ministry, he couldn't help but notice the irony of an institution dedicated to cutting-edge technology being housed in an architectural relic of the past. Built in the old Greco-Roman style, as many government buildings were, the ministry stood as an old, intimidating symbol of government power in the middle of a sprawling metropolis. It stood as a chilling stone structure, an emblem of the icy past, that housed the modern engine of society.

Entering the floor where the engineers worked, Viktor scanned the room as he usually did, seeing all the brightest minds hard at work on solving the problems of society. Yet for the first time, instead of marveling at this accomplishment of efficiency, Viktor felt irritation. He thought to himself, *This place is filled with all the most brilliant minds of our generation, being herded like cattle, always told what to do and what problems to solve. I wonder what problems they would solve if they were allowed to ask their own questions?*

Then Viktor saw his mentor, Lucius, sitting at work in his office. Viktor needed to tell him the results of the mission into the Woods.

Viktor walked into Lucius's office for the second time in as many days.

Lucius looked up from his desk.

"Well, well, well, you're finally here. Good morning, Viktor; it's nice to see you. How'd you sleep last night?" quipped Lucius.

"Well, as usual. What are we going to be doing today?" replied Viktor, completing the formality.

"Evidently a bit too well. But don't sweat it, you didn't miss much," teased Lucius. He smiled at Viktor. "How was your mission? Any takeaways?" asked Lucius, an innocent question that would lead to a blasphemous answer. And blasphemy had its consequences.

The mission into the Woods had changed Viktor's life. Yet, the change was heretical to the City, and Viktor knew it. He thought of how much more idyllic and colorful life was in the Woods in comparison to the drab, white-walled, cold office he stood in.

"It was good. The Woods is a scary place, so uncivilized, far inferior to our City," Viktor replied, sticking to the party line. He forced the words out of his mouth.

"That sounds about right. Now you have a better perspective on just how much HAPOC enhances life for us," Lucius replied.

"Yeah, the amount of uncertainty and unnecessary suffering out there is appalling. It's frightening to think that would be us without HAPOC." Viktor said all the right words but believed none of them. He added, "You've been out there too, right?"

Lucius replied, "Yes I have a very long time ago, on a mission just like yours. I agree with your assessment, though I recall there were a few things I was fond of."

Viktor perked up. Did Lucius also possibly share his views on the Woods? Would he be someone he could speak with on this? A confidante?

"Like what?" Viktor asked.

"It was interesting being without HAPOC. It was fun, exciting almost, to have to make all your decisions on your own. A bit daunting and challenging, of course, but it was fulfilling to know that I was able to do a lot of things completely on my own. Small things to be proud of. But, of course, I wouldn't want to live that way every day; it'd be way too dangerous, and I'd probably make so many suboptimal decisions without HAPOC."

So, Lucius had indeed experienced some of the same findings that I had about complete individual agency and the corresponding fulfillment.

"That was certainly interesting. We're imperfect, and HAPOC outclasses us by a wide margin, but it's still fun to use our own free will to make decisions sometimes," said Viktor, choosing his words carefully.

"Yeah, don't use it too much, though; you most likely will end up in a suboptimal situation. We're definitely better off not relying on free will. All it does is lead to suboptimality. Our brains aren't good enough to ensure an optimal outcome. That's why we have HAPOC," Lucius responded.

Taken aback by this sudden reversal to the party line, Viktor wanted to see if Lucius had any more to say on the subject that would align with his own views. "Do you think there can be value in suboptimality?"

Lucius replied, "Why yes, I'm glad you asked that. It's something so many in our City overlook. It can actually enhance our lives."

Viktor was encouraged by this response and smiled. "Yeah! I think so too. I had some bad experiences in the Woods, but they were momentary, and they only made me stronger in the long term. I mean, all the luxury and comfort that HAPOC provides does offer much hedonistic pleasure, but suboptimality has the potential to be very valuable to us!" Viktor remembered Hugo's words, and was echoing them now.

Lucius grinned widely back at Viktor. "You've got it—I was hoping you would. Now that you have, there's something I need to show you. Come along."

Lucius heaved his healthy but aging body out of his chair in a manner untypical of men his age and briskly walked out of the office.

As Viktor followed, he wondered if this had been the purpose of the mission all along? Was it some kind of test to see if Viktor would be enlightened enough to be exposed to whatever it was that Lucius was about to show him? Had he passed?

Lucius walked onto the engineering floor where all the other engineers were hard at work. Viktor followed closely behind, intensely curious. Lucius kept walking, out of the entire building, passing by the rigid and uncompromising exterior of the edifice.

"Where are we headed?" asked Viktor, unable to contain himself.

"Right there." Lucius pointed to the building adjacent to the one they had just exited.

It was a building much like their workplace—tall, gray, and uncompromising, yet also architecturally sound and efficient. Corinthian columns rose high from the ground and the facade was made similarly in the Classical style. Viktor knew what this building was. It was the Ministry of Optimality, the place from where the Overseer, the head of government and the supreme architect of the System, administered society.

Viktor wondered what this could mean. Maybe he had proven himself with his open-minded views on suboptimality—maybe now that he was recognized to have been enlightened, he would be lauded and introduced to the wise leaders of the City. Maybe he'd even get to serve in the Ministry of Optimality. He thanked Lucius in his heart for the opportunity. Or maybe. ...

They walked up the stony steps and into the Ministry of Optimality. At the top of the steps, a large, imposing, metallic door stood. Lucius allowed himself to be retinally scanned and soon after, the door opened. They entered, and the door slammed shut with a metallic clang.

They had entered into a rectangular chamber with high ceilings and walls of marble. Guards stood at the edges of the room and by the entryway. They each were dressed identically and stood robotically, not moving a muscle. Then Lucius spoke.

"This is him. Take him."

All of a sudden, the guards at the entryway where Lucius and Viktor stood sprung to life and seized Viktor by the arms, restraining him. Viktor struggled for a moment and then gave up, knowing that it was futile. Then it all dawned on Viktor. The mission was all a setup, a test of Viktor's faith in the System. But he had all but confessed to Lucius that he held different ideals, that he viewed suboptimality and free will in a positive light, and that he questioned the optimality of HAPOC.

Lucius turned to Viktor and spoke. "I'm sorry, Viktor. You failed your mission. You and your ideals have been corrupted. HAPOC had detected a high probability that you would be susceptible to the allures of chaos. So, we tested you. I had hope for you, but, as usual, HAPOC was correct. Now you'll see the Overseer." He then turned and walked out of the room.

The door closed again, and the guards led him forward into the bowels of the Ministry. Within Viktor, a pent-up rage grew that threatened to explode. The betrayal from his mentor Lucius stung, but he should have known. And now he was being led to the man who had orchestrated all of this and created the System that Viktor had believed in so firmly until yesterday—the Overseer. *I'm being led to the man who is the root cause of all of this. The man who has deprived us of free will and any adversity whatsoever.* This was his chance to confront the man.

CHAPTER XV

The hallway was white with high ceilings and a stark lack of features. As the guards escorted Viktor through the hall, he strode forward confidently, determined to fight the System at its very roots, starting with the man who helped pioneer it, the Overseer.

They kept walking until they entered a large chamber with a high marble dome. In the center was a chair, throne-like and white, and on that chair sat a man, large and intimidating. On the chair was emblazoned his title: "Overseer of HAPOC." The man moved. With a wave of his hand, the guards were dismissed, and Viktor was left alone in the grand chamber with the Overseer.

"So, this is our young prodigy. Please come closer. What has brought a prodigious young man like you so much trouble?" the Overseer began.

The Overseer, with a voice much more timid than his office would suggest, welcomed Viktor into the chamber. He was an elderly man, with a silver beard and gray hair on his scalp. His face was wizened by wrinkles but had the look of a man who was to be reckoned with. The hair on his head was combed neatly, and not a strand was out of place.

Viktor, taken aback by the cordiality of the Overseer, controlled the rage swelling inside him and walked slowly forward, replying, "Today, I discovered that my life is predetermined, preordained. There always is only one way forward because of HAPOC, because HAPOC has told me so."

The Overseer smiled and murmured, "My child, that's nonsense. HAPOC merely provides you with the best information with which to guide your own decisions. It's a tool—"

Viktor interjected, "HAPOC doesn't guide. It orders. I've seen it with my own eyes. HAPOC's way is the only way. I've double checked the code. HAPOC has the computing power to simulate all possible decisions and outcomes. What it comes out with is the only correct answer."

The Overseer raised an eyebrow, "Is that not a beautiful thing? Because of HAPOC, your generation is the most informed generation in the history of mankind. My generation can't say the same."

"Does HAPOC inform my decisions, or command them?" Viktor inquired.

The Overseer ruminated, gazing pensively at the grand marble ceiling. "Let me tell you a story. A story of my youth. Before HAPOC. I was born into a family much like yours—loving parents, suburban childhood, a precocious interest in algorithms. However, unlike you, Viktor, I have few unpleasant memories of my mother. One that I will never forget is watching her die before my eyes ..."

A tear streaked down the Overseer's face as he recalled the painful memory. A short pause followed, then the Overseer composed himself and continued with his story. "For, you see, my family has a rare but potentially fatal genetic defect. But there was no need for her to die. The doctors got it wrong: the wrong prescription, the wrong treatment. They spliced in the wrong gene to fix the defect. The new spliced gene only accelerated her death. The doctors weren't trying to kill her; they simply didn't know."

Now, the Overseer's voice shifted to a more triumphant tone. "The disease runs in my family. I have it too. So as to avoid a similar fate, to avenge my mother's unfortunate but preventable fate, to promote prosperity for the others around me, making my own small contribution to our civilization, and to ensure that no one would ever have to feel the pain that I felt ever again, I dedicated my life to developing HAPOC. And then one day, the breakthrough happened. It worked. I was the first to have my genetic code and biological makeup completely scanned by HAPOC—only natural given my scientific instinct. And with my genetic code in its system, it ran forty-two thousand potential gene-splicing treatments to cure my defect and ascertained the optimal one. Today, I stand before you in health. No doctors made mistakes in my case due to 'simply not knowing.' What was once a terrible disease that took a mother away from a young child is now nothing more than a mild nuisance, a five-minute gene therapy session every month. In a quite literal way, I owe my life to HAPOC. I owe my life to HAPOC informing my decisions. And I have spread its gifts with the world, enhancing the daily lives and activities of billions across the globe, at every moment."

Viktor felt a small twinge of pity for the Overseer, but quickly regathered himself. He replied bluntly, "There's no arguing that HAPOC saves lives and improves welfare, but it erodes the core of human life—the ability to make free choices. I haven't done anything of my own accord for my entire life. I have only ever asked HAPOC and listened, following its mechanical voice like a slave who knows no better."

"My dear boy, your desires are, we must agree, still your own. You have the freedom to choose what you want. To choose what you want HAPOC to help you with. HAPOC merely informs you on how to fulfill those desires in the best way." The Overseer gazed at the domed ceiling as he spoke. "If you want to vacation in New Boston, then HAPOC will simply tell you what the best flight, hotel, and travel plans are according to your preferences, but the decision and desire to vacation in New Boston is your own, not HAPOC's. HAPOC is your tool. It's there to help make your dreams reality. It's there to service you," reported the Overseer.

Viktor remained indignant. He glared with determination at the Overseer. Eyebrows furrowed and eyes focused, Viktor replied. "HAPOC knows what I desire better than I even do. It knows what activities release the most endorphins in my brain and what foods activate the richest taste buds. Are my desires really my own, or are they, too, preordained?"

"That, Viktor, is a fact of biology, not a reason to have an existential crisis. HAPOC or no HAPOC, those activities and foods are objectively what's best for you. HAPOC merely elucidates that. It identifies which activities your brain likes the best and what foods your tastes buds prefer. HAPOC is an identifier, not a determiner. Your genes are the determiner, whether those determinations are identified or not. Are your desires your own or are they given to you?"

Viktor responded, "Fine; for argument's sake, let's say my desires are my own, or a product of my own genes. Still, every desire I have maps to one action. An action decided by HAPOC. There's no other option. For HAPOC is always right. Through making me more informed and less uncertain, you have chipped away slowly at my ability to choose until now it's nonexistent."

"Nonsense, no one would ever characterize being given more information as having their freedom taken away. If you were deciding between going to the club or studying for a test, and I told you the expected value of how much studying for the test would boost your exam score, you would then proceed to tell me that I'm taking away your freedom? Nonsense."

The Overseer looked at Viktor like a child in need of a scolding and continued, "If you're conflating being more informed and certain with losing freedom, then you're sorely misguided. Taken to its extreme, your argument would imply that the most clueless of us all would be the freest." He shook his head chidingly. "Knowledge is a virtue, not a vice. And as for your options under the HAPOC system, let me ask you this: given a choice between the objectively optimal choice and any other choice, what should one choose one-hundred percent of the time?" the Overseer asked.

Viktor exclaimed, exasperated, "That's the problem! I want the right to be wrong! To be suboptimal!" Viktor could feel the air around him grow hotter as he grew more heated. Blood rushed through his body.

The Overseer waved his hand, as if swatting an imaginary fly, "What a completely nonsensical desire. If you know that one way is undeniably the best, why would you ever go any other way?"

"Because freedom of choice trumps payoff of outcome!" declared Viktor. "I am sick of being ramrodded into a singular choice."

The Overseer sighed. He got up out of his marble throne, and began to pace the room, embarking on a lecturing monologue. "Viktor, throughout all of human history, we have sought to be able to do things better, to learn more, to be better informed. Finally, because of HAPOC, we can now erase all uncertainty from any decision. We can finally find out the real truth in any instance. We can better avoid the pitfalls of indecision and wrong decisions than ever before. In any case, we can make decisions more precisely and accurately than any generation that came before us."

His eyes pierced through Viktor's as he lectured the young man.

"No more vacillation. No more hesitation. No more uncertainty. Only optimality." With each clause the Overseer swung his fist down in the air. "It's about getting what you truly want, what's best for you. Can't you see, we have reached the pinnacle of human knowledge? This is something generations of scientists have dedicated their lives to, and we have finally attained it. And now you object? You object to the privilege given you? To the work of those many thousands who came before you?"

Viktor, insulted by the condescension in the Overseer's voice, remarked, "Enough history lessons. Yes, I can now avoid the pitfalls of indecision and wrong decisions. But I am also now less free than ever before. It's more than the death of uncertainty; it's the death of free will!"

The Overseer quickly retorted, "Only the free will to be wrong. Here's another history lesson: In the archaic Christian tradition, free will was the reason that evil exists in the world. God gave humans free will, but humans used it to sin." He gesticulated wildly as he pontificated about the inadequacies of humanity, like a dictator giving a hateful speech.

"And it isn't so hard to see that, ever since HAPOC came into existence, or, as you more bluntly state, since free will was taken away, the world has become an infinitely better place. Free will only leads to suboptimality. We humans, myself included, are imperfect creatures. We are notoriously bad at figuring out what we want and what's good for us. Isn't it great that we now have a tool to compensate for those deficiencies? We need the information HAPOC provides us in order to live better, fuller lives. And besides, the loss of free will was simply a secondary effect, an externality. Our intent with HAPOC is and always was a genuinely benevolent one: to empower mankind with information like never before. To educate and to inform."

Viktor pleaded, his voice shaking yet loud. "I only ask for the ability to choose!"

The room tasted like iron.

"You ask for the right to choose wrong. The right to choose something that you know would lead to a worse outcome for yourself. The right to be completely irrational. The right to drag our society and our population toward suboptimality and chaos. And that I cannot allow. You see, the root of your so-called 'free will' is uncertainty. When there's no uncertainty, there's no other choice but the one that's certainly correct. Your 'free will' is simply a symptom of your imperfection, of your weakness, of your lack of information."

The Overseer returned to his throne, pleased with his explanation.

"However noble your intentions were, the fact remains that my free will, my essential ability to live life, has been seized. The road to hell is paved with good intentions," Viktor responded, gathering himself. He struggled to calm down and reassume his original cool, confident stance.

The Overseer scoffed.

"Is it really so essential? Before today, you were living a beautiful, happy life, just like the other billions of people in this paradise of a world that we have created. Your free will and your newfound self-awareness only detract from your human experience. Your lack of free will and awareness enhances it. And if that's the case, then you should logically realize that there's nothing special about free will. It adds nothing to your life but takes away significantly. Such a thing cannot be called essential. Instead, it should be called detrimental and unnecessary. You could do better without it. By definition, something like that is nonessential."

"No, the freedom to choose, even to err, is what gives life meaning. Only through hardship can we understand what joy is. If nothing is difficult, then how can anything be worth anything?" Viktor replied in a steady tone.

"Is that so? Because my life and the lives of almost all whom I oversee are filled with joys. Surely, we're all happier than you are in your current exasperated and sorry state. This feeling is definitely worth something to me. It enhances my life and makes me happier. The proof can be seen in my brain—if you were to measure the amount of oxytocin and serotonin my brain produces, it would be much higher than that of your brain, and the opposite would be true of our respective cortisol levels. Viktor, the joy I feel is very real, and I see no reason why having adversity accompanying that joy would enhance it."

"A chemical response isn't the same thing as true emotion. True emotion comes from true experiences. Things that require effort and earning, struggle, and grit," declared Viktor. He motioned as he spoke, raising his hand and forming it into a fist as he uttered the word "grit," like a philosopher lecturing an audience.

"Is that so? Then what's true emotion? The brain feels the chemicals. If the chemicals secreted by a 'true experience' are the same as what we can introduce into our bloodstream without all the negative aspects of your 'true experiences,' then what's the difference? You're simply subjecting yourself to unnecessary suffering," replied the Overseer.

"You've taken away the right to be wrong and the right to struggle for anything. When HAPOC takes away all uncertainty, not only is it taking away free will, it's also taking away the good fight. HAPOC hands you the answer to everything on a platter. Everything is given to you for free, nothing is earned—no one even has to do the tiniest bit of thinking or go through the smallest adversity because HAPOC solves it all. And once one comes to that realization, they will see the truth, and won't be able to go back to life under HAPOC."

"You're cursed by your newfound knowledge. See how unhappy it has made you? You would be better without it," replied the Overseer.

"No, I feel more fulfilled with it. You coddle an entire society, removing all barriers in sight. Without the rain there can be no rainbows. My experience feels truer, more fulfilling, than anything HAPOC could ever give me."

"Yet now you're the one in pain, whereas I'm the one in pleasure. You're not unique. I have the same knowledge that you have—I simply choose to ignore that knowledge because it would only detract from my life. And that's why I've kept it from everyone. So, their lives won't be detracted from, like yours has."

"Detracted? No. My life and my feelings feel true. The purpose of life isn't pleasure—we have a higher calling. Simply minimizing the pain and maximizing the pleasure won't do. I've experienced something, something good, something that you've prevented an entire society from ever experiencing," retorted Viktor.

"Let me ask you a simple thought experiment. It's a thought experiment formulated by a thinker of centuries past. I'd like you to imagine that an amazing machine exists that could simulate in your brain any experience you may desire, and that this simulation is so good that you cannot distinguish it from reality. Would you not sit in this machine forever? This is the thought experiment that has inspired HAPOC. We hope that one day, it will indeed become such a machine. For now, we cannot simulate the experiences perfectly, so we have settled for making sure the experiences happen in reality," said the Overseer.

Viktor stared, momentarily shocked that the Overseer had just admitted to building an entire society on such a concept, and that Viktor had toiled diligently to help the Overseer build it.

"Such a machine would be an abomination to who we are as human beings. Nothing would be true. Life would be replaced with sitting in a chair, motionless, just experiencing it vicariously through the machine," replied Viktor.

"Yet, you wouldn't know it. In your mind, you'd be doing everything your heart desired. Your 'true experience' is simply a means to an end. I'm offering you that end without the difficulty of the means," replied the Overseer.

"It's not a means to an end. It *is* the end. The goal is to experience something of value. And value cannot be ascribed to a thing without some struggle, some price. Things must amount to something. Must be worth something. Otherwise, life itself is valueless. What is life and what is experience worth if nothing is paid for it?" asked Viktor.

"You ask for too high a price. No one is willing to pay for what they can get for free. It's irrational," replied the Overseer. He rubbed his forehead wearily, clearly losing interest in the cycling conversation.

"The payment gives value to the object. The sacrifice ascribes value. With every effort we make, and with every second of time we spend, the object of our travails becomes more valuable. The value of something is given implicitly by what we put into it," said Viktor.

He continued. "The people I met in the Woods taught me the real value of a thing. It's the product of your work, your efforts, the adversity undertaken to achieve it."

"Ah, I see; so, you'd rather live in that uncivilized backwater than in our prosperous City," said the Overseer calmly. He stroked his beard. The Overseer didn't display any sense of surprise at this mention of the Woods.

Viktor replied, "It's not about the material items. We're surrounded here in the City by an endless supply of luxuries and comforts, yet no one here knows what it's like to earn something. No one knows of that feeling of fulfillment. Everything here is so focused on the corporeal. And while the Woods may not have the comforts we have here, it has something much more valuable: nourishment for the soul."

Viktor continued. "I only ask for the right to struggle— only then can life measure up to all that it can be."

The room was silent for a second. A tense feeling filled the air. Then, the Overseer snapped his fingers, and the sound echoed through the room. A moment later, the grand door opened, and armed men entered the chamber.

The Overseer stood. "Enough. If that's what you want, then so be it. I know what's to be done for you."

CHAPTER XVI

Viktor awoke. It was black. He didn't know where he was, or how he had gotten there. He tried to move but couldn't. Everything was quiet.

Suddenly, the Overseer's disembodied voice boomed in an ominous tone.

"Viktor, you are now in the simulation machine we ruminated on earlier. It indeed exists in our reality—a prototype, but it will soon be fully functional. Perhaps this machine will be the future, the next step after HAPOC."

The voice continued.

"Here, I can make you feel whatever sensation I choose. It's time for some education, for the purpose of helping you understand how privileged of a life you have had under HAPOC."

And with these words, Viktor's field of vision erupted into color. Harsh hues of red and blue flashed before his eyes. He felt pain. Heartache. Loss. Suffering.

Sensations flowed through his body as images darted through his mind. Viktor was in a field with emaciated and dead children all around him, victims of a failed agricultural policy. Starving survivors sought to cannibalize the dead in a desperate attempt to quench their unending hunger. And then Viktor felt it too—a pain in his stomach that felt like a thousand knives cutting into this abdomen.

Then, he saw his mother in the ward of a hospital, her lifeless corpse on a bed, the result of choosing an ineffective treatment option. He felt tears run down his face and a crushing sensation in his heart. He felt every single emotion of a boy who had lost his mother in childhood.

And then it was two weeks later. He was at his mother's funeral. Her decaying body was in an open casket. Her skin was pale though blackness crept up to its surface, evidence of the life having left her body. The sense of finality struck him, and he knew she was gone. An emptiness filled his heart. His spirit became devoid of joy, and he continued on into the abyss full of anger and sadness at the unfairness of the tragedy.

More scenes flashed before his mind. A city destroyed by rising sea levels due to ineffective choices made to combat climate change. His body being pummeled by the rushing water and his subsequent suffocation. A world destroyed by nuclear war, the result of a disastrous miscalculation by two warring nations. The radiation seared through his body as his skin slowly charred and his cells mutated into tumors. Though simulated, he bore the full physical and emotional brunt of each experience. Viktor lived through lifetimes of hardship and suffering in these few minutes.

Then, everything went black.

CHAPTER XVII

————

Viktor awoke again. He was no longer in a building. The pains had gone from his body. He could feel the caress of nature beneath him.

The sun shone directly overhead, brighter than any of the light-emitting diodes of the City. Viktor was on his back. Around his body he felt the soft embrace of grass. He sat up, and all he could see in front of him was greenery. The verdant colors once again filled the rods and cones in his eyes. He saw the green of the grass, the brown of the dirt, the blue of the sky, and the white of the clouds. On his skin, he could feel the sweet breeze again and through his nose he could smell the scent of the Woods. Viktor turned around, and saw the large, looming, gray gate separating the Woods from the City, the same one he had walked through with Alice.

Viktor looked back at the City.

Guards could be seen on the top of the walls, watching him. So, this is what the Overseer had done. Exile. He had been taken out of the City after his ordeal, banished to the Woods. In this way, the Overseer had been kind. The City had its way of life and the Woods had its own differing way of life. They were to remain separated. That was why the wall was so high. Viktor had rejected the City's way, and, in turn, the City had rejected him. It was an arrangement that benefited both parties.

No longer was Viktor surrounded by the perfection of the City. No more right angles at intersections, no more high-rises, no more HAPOC. No more limitless pleasure, no more avoiding the pain.

He would never see his parents again. No more autos would bring him wherever he needed to go. No more amenities would be provided at the click of a button or the utterance of a request. He would have to earn everything from now on. HAPOC would no longer be handing him the answer to everything. And all those horrors he had felt so vividly, they were all possible now. More roots would be in his path to trip him and more splinters would stab him.

There were doubts in Viktor's mind. HAPOC had indeed solved some of humanity's greatest problems. The artificial intelligence had prevented all those catastrophes the Overseer had shown him in the machine. In the City, there was no starvation, no nuclear war, no climate apocalypse, no grief, suffering, or heartbreak.

Viktor stood up. He decided he would welcome the challenge. The decision carried the same sense of finality as how he felt when he saw his mother's corpse—his old life, his old family, friends, and relationships were all now dead.

Despite his doubts, he pushed himself to embrace his new life. He had walked this path before, and he knew the way to Hugo's village. He started along the path.

It was time to chop wood.

Made in the USA
Middletown, DE
09 May 2021